# Dear Mr. President

# *Dear Mr. President*

■

# Gabe Hudson

Alfred A. Knopf   New York   2002

THIS IS A BORZOI BOOK
PUBLISHED BY ALFRED A. KNOPF

www.aaknopf.com

Knopf, Borzoi Books, and the colophon are registered trademarks of Random House, Inc.

Owing to limitations of space, notice of previous publication of stories can be found following the acknowledgments.

Library of Congress Cataloging-in-Publication Data

Hudson, Gabe.
Dear Mr. President : stories / by Gabe Hudson.
p. cm.
ISBN 0-375-41395-2
1. Persian Gulf War, 1991—Fiction. 2. Americans—Persian Gulf Region—Fiction. 3. War stories, American. 4. Soldiers—Fiction. I. Title.

PS3608.U543 D43 2002
813'.6—dc21                    2002020812

Manufactured in the United States of America
First Edition

*To my relentless mother and father*

Because I could not stop for Death—

—*Emily Dickinson*

# Contents

# The Cure as I Found It

■

I should probably start at the point where Fear Me crashed into my life. It was a Friday night and I was lying on the floor goofing around with Whiskers, waiting for Gloria to stop by after work. Whiskers and I were playing the shoelace game, which means I was jerking a shoelace around the floor and Whiskers was chasing the shoelace around the floor, trying to pin it down with his paws. Whiskers is an orange tabby I found in the trash can shortly after moving to Providence. I lifted the lid and there he was, lying on a pile of pizza boxes and empty milk cartons and fashion magazines and old computer cords, with his tongue lolling out of his mouth and a halo of flies buzzing around his head. And then at some point Whiskers stopped chasing after the shoelace, feigning boredom, and turned and looked at me with his one good green eye. "Meeooooow." I tussled his head. I laughed and said, "Hey, partner. Okay. Okay. Hold your horses." I popped open a can of tuna while he did cartwheels and pirouettes around his dish, shedding a small tornado of fur in the air. And it was then, as I was spooning the tuna into his dish, it was then that the sound of breaking glass exploded in my apartment.

I flew back to the bedroom where the noise had come from, and there on the floor, atop a salad of broken glass shards, was an old basketball. I figured someone just must have missed the basket, and in my head I was already trying to figure out if I should make them pay for the window and deciding that I should not, because accidents happen, and because of how much I love to play hoops myself, but then I realized the courts were a good hundred yards away, at least, and besides, my place was on the third floor. What the hell?

I felt my heart break into a jog.

I held the ball up to the light and noticed there was something written on it in Permanent Marker. YOU WUNT TO PLAY HOLMES? I read it again. YOU WUNT TO PLAY HOLMES? Suddenly a yellow bolt of realization flashed across my mind, and I dropped the ball and flung my head out the smashed window and peered down into the darkness. "Hey!" I shouted. "Leave me alone!" Someone in the street below started cracking up, and I jerked my head in the direction of the laughter, trying to make the scariest face I could.

But I could not see a thing.


Everybody's Gulf War Syndrome is a little bit different and in my case I knew something wasn't right when, two months after rotating back to the world from Desert Storm, all the hair on my head suddenly turned completely white. Still, for the next couple weeks afterward, I went around trying to pretend nothing was wrong with me, tried to tell myself that this was just a temporary setback and that my old brown hair would return in no time. How could it not? I mean I was what, twenty-four, just about to turn twenty-five, still a kid in every sense of the word.

Then all my hair fell out. I was suddenly bald. This was more than a blow, this was something like having my hands chopped off and stuffed in my mouth, to be bald. I do not care what people say: to lose your hair is the highest sort of tragedy, and as a result I felt myself slipping under fast, felt myself being sucked down irretrievably into the torturous pit of darkness and despair that every bald man must secretly endure.

So I changed my line of reasoning quick, acknowledging that my hair was not coming back, not my old brown hair or my new white hair, and tried to tell myself that my new bald head was cool, different, sexy even (besides, I still had my youth), at least that is what my girlfriend, Gloria, said. "My beautiful old man," she would coo. I even told myself that I wouldn't accept my old hair if it tried to grow back in, that I would shave it all off. Hair was stupid, anyway. Any old schmuck could have hair, but not anybody could be bald, etc., etc.

But then in late February, a couple weeks after my twenty-fifth birthday, I mysteriously sprained my wrist while shooting a lazy jump shot in the playground. The second I released the ball it felt like someone had smashed my wrist with a hammer, and that's when I went to see Dr. Himmons. He immediately ran a bunch of tests and X rays, and a week later I was back in his office for the results. Dr. Himmons told me to sit down, but before I could sit down he held up the X rays and I fainted. My skeleton was riddled with holes. It looked like a worm had been eating and tunneling through my bones. When I came to, Dr. Himmons was weeping and holding my head in his hands, and muttering, "I'm sorry, Larry. Oh my gosh, I'm so sorry." Then he explained to me that I had Gulf War Syndrome, and my particular strain of Gulf War Syndrome was disintegrating my bones at a massive rate and if things kept up this way every bone in my body would be gone within the year and there was nothing he could do. I was going to be the human blob.

About a half hour after the ball came crashing through my window, I called Gloria at work and told her what had just happened, and suggested, given the circumstances, that maybe us getting together that night wasn't such a good idea. She whis-

pered, "I'll be right there." Ten minutes later there was a knock
at the door, and when I opened it Gloria pushed past me and
said, "Show me the window! I can't believe this! That son of a
bitch! His ass is grass! Show me the goddamn window!" Later
that night, after we had swept up the broken glass and coaxed
Whiskers out from under the couch, she started rubbing me
down with lotion, trying to ease the pain in my bones, which had
left me feeling, well, rusty. I was draped in bed on my stomach,
with my arms spread wide, like Jesus. Gloria ran the heel of her
palm up my spine.

"Mmmm. That feels good, Gloria. Keep doing what you're
doing."

When I got back from Saudi, this was about a year and a half
ago now, I got my discharge from the army, packed my stuff, and
moved from San Francisco out here to Providence. I was living off my V.A. checks, and I was going to start at Brown in the
fall, where I would be a Religious Studies major. In high school
I was a National Merit Scholar, and my senior year I'd been
accepted to Brown on early admission, but then at the last second, because of an overrated epiphany arrived at after reading
way too much Hemingway, I elected not to go, eschewing the
sterile classroom for life: which translated into six long years as a
rifleman in the army, but now I was ready to pick up where I'd
left off, so when people asked me what I wanted to be, I'd say, "A
shepherd." I pictured myself, down the road, as an old man sitting on top of a mountain, alongside my devoted herd of billy
goats, with a blue-gray beard that fell to my bare toes.

While we'd been sweeping up the glass, Gloria had been
needling me, trying to get me to do something in retaliation to
Fear Me and his crew for the thing with the basketball. And now,
as she rubbed me down, she started in again.

She said, "Come on, Larry. Think about it. Fucking take
them out. Put this thing to rest."

Gloria was my Super Good Thing. I met Gloria the first day I moved into the neighborhood, I went down to the Deli Grocery, and she saw my high and tight haircut and instantly started flirting with me from behind the register, asking me about the army. "Nice butt," she'd said. And sure, Gloria was a little cheeky, but her life has not been easy and deep down she is an angel with a heart of pure gold, and she makes all this other crap worth it. Gloria was a ballet prodigy until she was ten, and her instructor, Jacques, was always telling her that she was going to show the world, but then one time, during a performance of *The Wizard's Pond,* Gloria leapt, and when she landed on the "magic lily pad" her head jerked back as if someone had yanked it with a rope and she fell down. She had given herself whiplash. It turned out that her right leg had grown an inch longer than her left leg, and in the next year her right leg would grow another two inches, and in that same year Gloria would be kicked out of the ballet studio and botch her first of many suicide attempts. Today, though, you would never know any of this, unless you looked closely and noticed that her right boot heel is three inches taller than the left.

I turned my head to the side. "Give it a rest, okay, Gloria? Just forget about it. Kids get drunk and do things. Stop trying to make it into a big deal."

"Look, that's the dumbest thing I ever heard," Gloria said. "You think Fear Me's going to forget about it? You embarrassed him in front of his crew. This is his hood."

Fear Me was the neighborhood thug. Fear Me had the words *Fear Me* tattooed across his chest in big gothic letters. He had fierce blue eyes and a shaved head, and one of those wallets that has a big chain dangling from it, and once in broad daylight I'd seen him take a crap on the hood of a blue Chrysler stopped at a red light. Gloria had gone to elementary school with Fear Me and she said his real name was Donald.

"Hey," she said. "You were the one who had to dunk it. So now you've got to handle this."

I had gotten in a scuffle with Fear Me and his crew on the court the other day. We had been playing a pretty beasty game of full court, and the score was tied and it was game point. Everyone was sweating and yelling and playing extra-tight D, and then at some point, Fear Me dribbled through my team kamikaze-style and went up for what looked to be an easy two. But he did not see me. I came out of nowhere. I ran and leapt up behind him.

I stuffed Fear Me's shot and then scooted down the court and scored the game winner, and I guess I could have just laid it up, but instead I showboated a little bit and dunked it. I did a three-sixty dunk. I hung on the rim, and shouted, "Yeah!" He came galloping up behind me and shoved me the second my feet touched the ground. He said, "You fouled me, bitch. You got a problem, soldier boy? Huh?" Finally, I had to say, "Hey. I'm sorry, man. I didn't mean to foul you. I don't want any trouble."

And now Gloria was rubbing my shoulder blades, digging in with her thumbs. I rolled over onto my back and looked at her. "There's some things you just don't understand, Gloria. Trust me. I've dealt with—"

"You were a rifleman in the army for fuck's sake. You blasted those Iraqis at Al Mutlaa Ridge. Don't pretend like you didn't wax those guys. You want to know what you should do. Go hunt down these punks and cut all their tongues out and make a necklace with their tongues. Then we'll see who gets the last word."

I sighed. I was starting to regret that I ever told Gloria about the day my battalion took Mutlaa Ridge, how we clashed with the Iraqis fleeing back to Baghdad, how the Iraqis turned and took a stand on the ridge's high ground. Our objective was to pinch them off, lock them in—this was Schwarzkopf's famous Left Hook Maneuver, which would cinch the victory for the Allied Forces. This all happened along the highway in Kuwait that would come to be known as the Highway of Death. What can I say? I went over to Saudi crazy and thirsty for blood. I thought I could justify my life by taking someone else's, that I would be entering The Great Dialogue of War that man has been having ever since the beginning of time, that war was, in a sense, the ultimate form of divinity. So two days after G-day, which is what the media kept calling the first day of the ground war, when it became official that the Marines had secured Kuwait, my platoon of mech riflemen and three others charged over the desert in Bradley Fighting Vehicles.

Down there in the hull of the Bradley, we were getting jostled around on the benches and I remember I closed my eyes and for a split second I felt as if I was eight years old again, crammed in the back of Danny Gordon's mom's Dodge Caravan, heading to our Saturday soccer game, only this was no Dodge and Danny Gordon's mom was nowhere near this madness: this was an LAV powered by a 275 horsepower General Motors engine, and above us our gunner, Haden Fark, manned the 25mm Bushmaster cannon, ripping giant gashes in the Iraqi T-55s and T-62s that tried to stop our onslaught. I could hear Fark yelling, "That's right, Dr. Fark is in the house! The roof is on fire! That's right, we don't need no water, let the motherfucker burn!" Fark was also using his AN/TPQ-36 Firefinder radars, and each time an Iraqi shell exploded in our vicinity his computer would instantly map out its virtual arc on the screen and track back the coordinates of the shell's origin, and then he would rocket off an M-1093A3 self-propelled howitzer, blasting the Iraqi fool who was lobbing shells from a distance. The explosion of the howitzer erupting from our Bradley threatened to knock my ears off my head, and through my periscope I caught a glimpse of the red leering sun, obscured by the black haze billowing from the burning wells, as we crashed through Al Manaquish oil fields.

Our platoon leader, Riggins, shouted, "Charge! Charge! Charge!" Still dazed, I leapt out one of the personnel hatches, and we fanned out and hit the sand in a prone position, sighting in on the Iraqis firing from the windows of the police post up on the ridge. I clicked my M-16 on burst and blindly let the sparks fly. I couldn't see shit. There was a bright flash in one of the windows on the third floor of the police post, and an RPG rocket zoomed into our Bradley, blowing a charred hole in the side of it, and Fark popped out of the gunner's hatch and scrambled back to fuel and logistics in the rear. Bobby D. was the first one up, and he sprinted forward and stumbled over a trip wire and was suddenly blown thirty feet upward with his legs pumping the air beneath him as if he was on a StairMaster. Screaming Iraqis came charging out of some scrub brush off to the right. A bullet blew by my ear. I saw Trigger and Boogaloo drop dead without a peep. Everyone scattering everywhere at once. There was a high-pitched whine, and Riggins, who was basically right next to me, went up in a ball of flames. We had to cross the highway and get to the police building on the other side. People were screaming, "Go! Go!" I let out a bloodcurdling yell and scurried through the smoke and up the ridge.

On my way up I sprinted across that godforsaken Highway of Death and landed facefirst in a deep ditch on the other side, and when I glanced up there were two Iraqi soldiers perched on their rucksacks, in the middle of eating their breakfast by a Sterno fire, except suddenly a pair of boots stepped into my line of sight, and then the snubbed snout of a .45 pistol was squashing my nose flat to my face. My eyes, focused on the tip of the pistol, crossed. I was gasping for air, and the sounds of the battle seemed a million miles away. A thick Arabian-English voice, presumably belonging to the boots, said, "Well well well. What do we have here? Looks like this little birdy flew too far from his nest. Have you come on behalf of America to do some more of your Nation Building? No, you have come to negotiate the price of oil, I suppose? Do you know the price of oil, Mr. America?"

I rolled and swung the blade of my K-bar into the side of

Boots's right knee, and his pistol jerked down and went off. I saw his left boot toe explode in a gush of flesh and blood, and he screamed. I was already on my feet and I hurled a smoke grenade toward the other two soldiers, who were scrambling for cover. I leapt up on the sandy wall of the ditch, climbing higher and higher. Boots was hopping around on one foot, shouting and shooting bullets into the air, one of which nicked my foothold. I landed on the back of one of the soldiers and planted my teeth in his right ear. He yelled, "Arrrghhhh!" Then he stumbled backward and my head smashed against something and my vision was lit up with stars and I fell off him, taking the ear with me. In a daze, I got to one knee.

I spit the ear out of my mouth and glanced at my hand and saw the pistol in it. I must have grabbed it from Ear Man's belt when I fell off. So I stayed on that one knee and blew all three of those bastards away. I put a round in each of their chests. It was too easy. I shouted, "That's the price of oil, cocksucker!" and then flew up out of the ditch and onto the police post.

Gloria was rubbing my kneecaps and shinbones now. "Gloria? Remember what I told you," I said. "I'm trying to forget everything that happened to me in Saudi. You promised you wouldn't bring it up again."

But Gloria wouldn't let it go. She exploded. "You can't pretend like that ball didn't come through this window. Everybody in the neighborhood already knows. The word's out, Larry."

I suddenly got the feeling that Gloria had been running her mouth.

I sighed again. "Can you just hold me?" I asked her.

The expression on her face changed instantly. She melted.

"Sure, baby," she whispered.

And then she put her arms around me and started to cuddle. But before I knew what was going on, she had mounted me and we were suddenly making love. She was really working herself into a frenzy, bouncing up and down with her back arched, and her hands were grabbing the skin on my chest hard, and it seemed as if she had no idea that I was even there, except I guess I was wrong because right before she came Gloria threw back her head and her red hair exploded behind her and she gasped, "Oh G.I.! G.I.!"

The next day was Saturday. And, like we did every Saturday afternoon, Gloria and I sauntered down to the antique store on Wickenden Street.

"How much for that?" I said.

The wall-eyed guy manning the jewelry case grinned and said, "A special deal today for the bald gentleman," and then he winked at Gloria. What I bought from this man was a sterling silver ring, on which was mounted a dancing ballerina in a tutu. The ballerina had her arms up in a diamond over her head, and it was gorgeous. On Gloria's finger, it practically came to life.

"For *my* ballerina," I said, as I slipped the ring on.

Gloria did an awkward curtsy.

She said, "I was really good, you know."

"You still are," I said. "Let's see something."

So Gloria started leaping around the store. She was humming under her breath, turning and twirling, and a couple customers stopped to watch. She was even humming a couple lines from *The Wizard's Pond,* and that is when I noticed the beads of sweat pop out on her forehead. She was totally focused, fueled on by her will, her spirit, her passion. The wall-eyed guy said, "Wow. Will you look at that." Then she twisted her ankle and fell on her butt, and for a second, I thought she was going to cry, but instead she started laughing, so I ran over and fell on top of her, and then we were both laughing.

Five minutes later when I couldn't get up off the ground I wasn't laughing.

"These crappy bones are going to be the death of me," I said. "I can't move. Christ. Fuck this."

"What? Like you're not some kind of badass warrior? *Please*," said Gloria, reaching to help me up. "We'll find a cure for this. You're too much of a man to let this get you down."

Then: "Come on, let's get some milk. You'll walk it off."

And for the rest of that sun-splashed afternoon, we strolled arm in arm, battered but proud. Then, before I knew it, the sun had dropped and the moon was up, and Gloria and I were standing on the stoop in front of her building.

We had just finished a passionate kiss, and I said, "Well, baby?"

She giggled. "Do you want to come up and make me your prisoner of war? I think I've got some rope."

I put my arms around her. "Gloria, look. I really enjoy making love to you. But I want you to understand that I respect you as a woman. Tonight though, I just want to get some rest, okay?" And then I gave her a long, slow, gentle kiss, and I turned and strolled off into the night air, leaving her in a state that I could only imagine as breathless.

I passed a street clown and dropped a dollar in his hat.

As I came up my street, I suddenly stopped whistling. Because about twenty feet away, I saw Fear Me and his crew in front of my building in a circle, laughing and hooting and dancing around. When I got a little closer I saw Mrs. Tunolli in the middle of the circle, and they were dangling her mail up where she couldn't reach it from the wheelchair, and she was turning and turning and saying "Shame on you" and "Where are your mothers?"


The simple fact of the matter is that war makes people commit horrible acts. And it is hard to get into Heaven when you have committed horrible acts, so ever since the war I have been practicing getting into Heaven through visualization, because if you see something first, envision it happening in your mind ahead of time, there is a lot better chance that it will happen in reality. This is something my marksman instructor, Sergeant Barrow, taught me in boot camp, out on the firing range in Fort Leonard Wood. It was regal to march out to the range in your shooting jacket, singing old army songs as the sun rose over the hills and broke like an egg yolk: the righteous cadence of our boots on the tarmac, the deep soulful chorus of our voices, the sense that these were ancient songs, ancient rituals. I could feel then, just as I did when I lay in bed at lights out and listened to "Taps," the ghosts of past American wars, the great wars and astounding sacrifice of our fathers and grandfathers. Then it was time to pop off our M-16s at the human-shaped targets, all of us lying in the prone position along the shooting line, and the instructors pacing back and forth among us in safari hats. These guys were wizards, and behaved with class and reserve, as if their dedication to the accuracy of the round would guide them in all things of life, and it was Sergeant Barrow who taught me to actually see the round ripping a hole in the bull's-eye before I squeezed the trigger, and it worked. I shot expert on qualifying day.

So before I go to bed each night, I visualize myself ascending from earth and passing through the Golden Gates. I see myself as a perfectly round ball, with no bones, a flesh bag. I have gigantic, white-feathered wings on my back that are pumping the air. Strangely, I always have a beak instead of a mouth, and since I do not have any bones, the beak slides around all over my body. But the beak does not keep me from talking. I talk with the beak. I talk to Heaven's Doorman with my beak. The Doorman is a big guy dressed in a tuxedo, and the tuxedo has the arms cut out and you can see the word *love* tattooed on each of his forearms. He has a receding hairline and bad teeth.

As I hover there in front of the Golden Gates, I say, "Come

on. Give a guy a break. I'm sorry for what happened at Al Mutlaa
Ridge, it was my duty, and truly I didn't want to kill those guys. I
was scared. I did what I thought I had to do, and besides, back
then I wasn't even sure that God existed. But now I'm sure. Isn't
that some sort of redemption? The fact that now I am absolutely
certain? So what do you say? Let me in there. Listen to me. You
don't understand. I absolutely have to get in there." And then, in
the visualization, the Doorman bares his big snaggletooth smile
and steps aside and extends his arms in invitation, and says, "Of
course, Larry. I know you have a good heart, and that sometimes
things slip out of control. Life's been hard enough as it is. Go
ahead. Get on in there."

But then other times, and this is not intentional, because
it feels as if I lose control of my mind when this happens, the
Doorman frowns, and says, "What do you take me for? Larry,
you've got to pay for killing those Iraqi soldiers. Truth be told,
they weren't even going to hurt you; they were just having fun,
and now their children are fatherless. You're a murderer, plain
and simple. Don't try to get out of it, the rules are the rules, and
I can't make an exception for you, because if I do that, then I'll
have to start making exceptions for everyone. You know, you're
not the first person to try and pull this stunt. It wasn't that long
ago that Hitler was up here saying the exact same thing, and so
I'll tell you the same thing I told him. The standard is there for a
reason. It's part of the system, and the system works. Otherwise,
next thing you know everyone will be getting in, and then after
that what's the point in even having a Heaven?," and with that
the Doorman quickly claps his hands three times and my wings
suddenly disappear and I begin to fall.

So one of the thugs, this long, brown, greasy-haired guy in a
hockey jersey that said EAT MY PUCK, slapped Mrs. Tunolli
across the face, and her dentures popped out of her mouth. Her

mouth instantly collapsed, and Eat My Puck said, "Jesus, lady. God, you're ugly."

And you have to give Mrs. Tunolli some credit here, because she reached in her bra and whipped out a mace canister and shot a jet stream into Eat My Puck's eyes. She said, "Make mat, mou monumamitch." The thug crumpled to his knees and started screaming, "Ohmygod! I can't see! I can't see!" One of the other guys started laughing and said, "I guess she showed you!"

Fear Me cuffed the laugher on the head and said, "Shut up, you idiot." Everything got quiet. "Now listen here, you bitch," he said, turning on Mrs. Tunnoli, and he pushed the wheelchair over sideways with the sole of his shoe so that Mrs. Tunnoli spilled out of the chair and onto the ground. "Time to say good night." Fear Me reached to pull something out of his belt, and I caught a glimpse of something silver.

And that is where I stepped in.

"Hi guys. Anybody here thirsty?"

They just looked at me like what the hell.

Then I smashed the milk carton I had been holding into Eat My Puck's mouth, and white exploded everywhere. He tried to yell, but he sounded confused. Fear Me and the others started to close in on me and I knew I was done for. Fear Me actually said, "You're a dead man."

I heard the sound of a screeching whistle pierce the night. *Shhhhrt-shhhhrt-shhhhrt.* There was a flashlight beam dancing around, and I glanced up and spotted two cops running at us, and one of them was squawking into his walkie-talkie. "Code Four! Code Four! We've got a Code Four on Hope Street!"

Fear Me said, "Five-O."

The thugs evaporated.

I took that as my cue. I ran.

▪ ▪ ▪

I ran all the way to Gloria's place and collapsed on her doorstep, panting. Gloria opened the door and gasped, "Larry. What's amatter? What happened?" I told her how Fear Me had been hanging around in front of my building, waiting for me.

"Jesus," she said. "Oh God, baby, are you okay? Here, let's get you cleaned up."

I spent most of that night lying next to Gloria, staring at the ceiling, burning a hole in it, letting my mind turn the options over and over, then around three, I shook Gloria and said, "I have an idea. Let's get the hell out of Providence. Let's go somewhere new and start all over."

Gloria sat up in bed and scratched her head. "What are you talking about, Larry?" She yawned.

I could feel the moon outside the window smiling in on me.

"To Montana," I said. I explained to her that I had an old army buddy, Fletcher, who worked as a guide on a ranch up there. He took city people on horse rides through the mountains. Right before we shipped out of Saudi, Fletcher told me I could show up there any time, that he would get me work. I told Gloria about the beautiful ranch on the mountain we would live on, with the river that ran right through it, and how we could take the Greyhound and be there in two days. "Just imagine," I said. By the time I finished she was beaming.

"Yeah," she said, and broke into a grin. "Yeah. Okay. Let's do it." We talked, hatching out our new plan. Gloria would go to work in the morning, for her last shift, which went until 11:00, collect her check, and then we would meet at the Greyhound station at 12:00. The next morning when we stepped out the front door of her building the birds were singing. "All right, sweets," she said, and patted my butt, "I'll see you at twelve on the nose."

▪ ▪ ▪

The minute I got back to my place I knew something had gone wrong again. The door was slightly open, and I pushed through and stopped and gasped. All the windows were smashed out and there were basketballs scattered all over the floor. A cardinal had gotten inside my place, and when it saw me it started to fly up, banged its head into the ceiling, and then fell to the floor. It did this over and over and over. Then as I started to pick something up I saw it. Written on the wall in Permanent Marker was this: IF YOU WUNT YOUR KITTY COME AND GET IT. My mind started to race through the possibilities. Whiskers hanging from a rope with a broken neck. Whiskers floating facedown in the bathtub. I rushed around the apartment in a panic. Each time I flung open a cabinet my heart was full of hope, but Whiskers was nowhere to be found. Whiskers was gone. And that is when I went into full combat mode. I donned my desert cammie fatigues. I quickly painted my face with war paint. I hooked a grenade to my belt.

The first thing I noticed when I stepped out on the street was that the sun looked like a bright wet marble up in the sky, and the second thing I noticed was that I was having trouble walking. My Gulf War Syndrome was really acting up. It was all I could do to get my knees to bend, and I knew I looked like a robot. I checked my watch: 10:27. Farther down the street I could see Fear Me and his crew shooting hoops on the court, and I set off. As I got closer, I saw Fear Me go up and dunk the ball so hard the backboard rattled. There were high fives everywhere. Then I was standing at the edge of the court. Fear Me looked up, and his face fell into a grin. He said, "Looky what we have here."

They all looked up. "Hey," said Eat My Puck, joining in. "It's G.I. Joe."

I heard Mrs. Tunolli's voice. "Get out of here. Save yourself. Go get the police."

I turned toward the voice and saw Mrs. Tunolli. She was buried up to her neck in the sandbox. Off to the right of her were the monkey bars. She was a talking head.

"Oh nooo," Fear Me said, with scorn. "Don't leave, G.I. Joe. Silly boy. It's time for a rematch." He hurled the ball at me as if it had been shot out of a cannon. At the last second, I raised my hands to my chest and caught it calmly, as if to say, You are going to have to do a whole lot better than that if you want to live another day. But the second I felt the ball in my hands, my stomach dropped out on the court, and all the colors of the world began bleeding together. This was no basketball. It was Whiskers. Dead Whiskers in my hands. His limbs were gone. Patches of fur were missing. He smelled burnt. But there was his face, it was undeniable, and his one good green eye was still open, glazed over, looking up at me, as if to say, Where were you, partner?

"He he he," said Fear Me. "Meooow."

That is when I heard it: a long, sorrowful cry coming from very, very far away. It was some kind of horrible, piercing animal sound of agony. I looked up at the sky, and in that moment I realized the voice was my own.

Fear Me stepped up waving a sawed-off screwdriver, like a flag, and he said, "Come here, bitch," and then he danced in and expertly nicked my right cheek with it. I felt the teardrop of blood rise up on my face. He said, "Game over, soldier boy. Now your punk ass is going to pay."

The world was a merry-go-round.

I reached down deep into my madness. I was back at Mutlaa Ridge, the heat, the sand, the dizziness of death everywhere. I could hear Riggins shouting, "Charge! Charge!" I kicked Fear Me in the nuts and judo-flipped him on the ground. I leapt on top of him and punched him, cracked his jaw. Out of the corner of my eye, I saw a cop car pull up and two cops leap out and start bounding toward us. I glanced at my watch: 11:02. If I started running right now, I could probably get away and still meet Gloria in time.

I spotted Whiskers at the free throw line, and without giving it another thought I brought down my fist for the deathblow. In that second, Fear Me reached up in a quick snake move and yanked the pin out of the grenade on my belt. Then his eyes slanted in a smile and the next thing I knew my ears filled with the loudest noise I have ever heard, and I was suddenly being lifted up by a hot wave of air, up, up, and away from the earth and straight toward the clouds. Ahead in the distance, I could see the Doorman waving furiously, as if to say, "Okay, Larry. Okay, hurry, hurry. Come on, come on."

# Cross-Dresser

■

## The Written Testimony
## of Captain Jeffrey Dugan,
## 418ᵗʰ Squadron, Bandit #573

My name is Captain Dugan and at the request/demand of Dr.
Barrett, I am writing all this down. She says that only if I write all
this down will she be able to make a strong case for me to her
superior, Dr. Hertz. I have never actually seen this Dr. Hertz,
and so I have to take Dr. Barrett at her word that this Dr. Hertz
even exists. Otherwise, Dr. Barrett says, if I do not write down
my side of it, then legally they will have no choice but to keep me
here at the neuropsych ward at Holloman AFB, because she said
that a sane man has nothing to hide, whereas a crazy man is full
of secrets. To which I said, "Well, I'm sure as hell not crazy."
That's when she pushed this pencil and paper across the table
and said, "So prove it."

　　If I am to do myself justice, then I suppose I should start with
a thesis remark, and so here it goes: This world is strange, and to
me it is all very sinister and miraculous. If you don't agree with
me now, perhaps you will agree with me by the time you are
done reading this. Before I begin it's important to me that I
establish credibility, which means I want to say that I'm not
nearly as dumb as I look, because the truth is that how I look is

not who I really am (and I'm just not saying this because I'm short either). Probably other people have this secret too, that how they look is not who they really are, though sometimes I forget about this until I look in the mirror and then I'm like, "Oh God, not him again. There must be some mistake." But then I'm like, "Okay, what the hell, might as well: I mean it's not like I have a choice or anything."

Then I get in my F-117A Stealth Fighter, which I call Gracie, and fly up into the sky and kill people. Or at least I have, in the Persian Gulf, for which I was awarded the Silver Star, and I'm sure I'll have to kill some more people when I get out of here. Word on the base right now is Somalia's going to be the next hot spot. This is what I do for a living, and I try to have fun with it, since it's my job. I zoom around the earth in a sleek, black weapon of mass destruction, and I'd be lying if I didn't admit that it's a serious rush to be in the cockpit, because when I'm up there in the sky it's like I'm straight out of God's head, a divine thought inside a divine thought bubble, totally invisible.

Except that day when I got my ass shot out of the sky in Iraq and crashed Gracie in the desert. Right in the middle of a ramshackle military compound where I was taken as a POW and sadistically tortured by a one-eared man named The Mule. I didn't feel so invisible then.


Here is where I should mention my curse. This will explain some things. I was born with a gift. Or a curse depending on how you look at it. It's my dreams. My dreams let me see into the future. I know it sounds bizarre, but as proof to support this claim I'll tell you that three nights ago I had a dream in which I saw myself wearing a dark blue dress and red high heels (just like I am now) and sitting in a padded room with one arm handcuffed to a chair (just like I am now), writing a document that started, "My name is Captain Dugan and at the request/demand of Dr. Barrett, I am writing all this down." I should also probably mention that that dream had a happy ending because in that dream Dr. Barrett read over my statement proclaiming that I was innocent (which is the same thing I shouted when I felt the MP's tranquilizer dart stick in my hip) and then in the dream Dr. Barrett let me return to active duty (just like you will after you read this) after concluding that if anything I was merely compassionate to a fault, completely sane, and that I am a victim of my wife's vindictive, ridiculous accusation that I am some sort of sicko transvestite pervert.

The mission was supposed to be simple. A routine sortie, clear skies, fly low and blow up some oil refineries south of Nukhayb, and then get the hell out of there. I was sitting around with Captain Jibs and Colonel Cowry under the tent, this was in Khamis Mushait, trying to stay out of the heat, sipping on a cold one when I got the word. I remember downing my beer and standing up in the same motion, and then slamming the bottle on the table and looking at Jibs and Cowry with a grin and saying, "Back in a jiff, boys. Desert Storm calls." Then I hopped in Gracie and hit the wide Arabian sky. Well, when I came up on the oil refinery below me, I saw three Iraqi soldiers jumping up and down on barrels, waving white flags attached to sticks.

I let them have it. I swooped down and dropped a GBU-10 bomb, and my stomach was lit up with that smoky, mystical sensation you get when you kill something, which is virtually indescribable, though I can say for sure that it's the only time I can feel God really watching me: it's a good way to make Him sit up and take notice. And so there I was, basking in God's gaze, the wreckage smoking below me, when that son-of-a-bitch Iraqi fighter dropped in out of nowhere and tried to kill me, shooting my tail wing to tatters.

Gracie skittered forward among the clouds like a bumper

car. I was dazed. I smelled smoke. The Emergency Gear Extension handle was stuck. Then I tried to duck and roll, but Gracie was shimmying all over the place and I was in a spin, streaking toward the earth like a comet, and I watched in horror on the Multi-Function Display as the desert's giant yellow jaws rose up and then opened wide and swallowed me whole.

When I came to I was strapped in a chair with a lightbulb hanging over my head. There were cracks of sunlight coming through the bamboo walls. After blinking a few times I saw that I was in a small hut with three Iraqi soldiers. This was the place I would come to call The Shack. The soldiers were smoking and laughing about something, and one of them had his hands up in front of him, squeezing the air, like there were breasts. Then the one squeezing the air heard me moan and after glancing in my direction put two fingers in his mouth and whistled loud through the tiny barred window in the door. The door swung open and a small man with one ear walked directly up to me and cracked my jaw with a bully stick. My jaw was instantly dislocated, and I toppled over with the chair to the floor. Through the scream trapped in my head I heard the men laugh, and then the one-eared man said, "Hello. My name is The Mule. I have some questions for you. You will answer, no?"

I gasped for air. It felt like my mouth had been knocked up into my forehead. I tried to say something, and the top of my head opened up. I slowly squirmed forward a few feet, knees and elbows, dimly aware that the soldiers were watching my progress with detachment, and I heard one of them chuckle and mutter, "Americana." Finally I pushed my jaw hard up against a wall and then clink, with the sound of a camera shutter, my jaw popped back into place, and the relief flooded up my spine in waves of ecstasy. The relief never really went away after that. So that two hours later when The Mule struck me across the jaw for what seemed like the hundredth time I was almost, but not quite, grateful.

Instead I spit out some teeth.

From there on out it's mostly a blur. Because of the pain, I only remember images and flashes, smells, and, finally, the taste of blood in my mouth. The Mule wanted me to make a propaganda videotape.

The Mule said, "If you ever want to see your family again."

The Mule said, "This is not too much to ask. You will be a movie star."

The Mule said, "I am losing my patience, Lieutenant Dugan."

The Mule said, "That looks like it hurts, Lieutenant Dugan."

I didn't say anything. I kept my mouth shut, but not because I was feeling patriotic, because to tell the truth I couldn't care less about my country at that moment, but because I was sure that if I did it, make the videotape, then they wouldn't have any more use for me and they would kill me.

The Mule whipped out this handheld Sears Craftsman electric drill. I had my focus back. He revved the trigger a few times and the drill made a squealing sound. Then he walked over to me and placed the drill to the back of my head. "Perhaps now you make the video?"

I gave him a look. I said, "Please don't do this."

The Mule smiled. "Have it your way, Lieutenant Dugan."

"Please," I said. "No."

Then I felt the bit of the drill push hard against my skull. It was very quiet, and I could see everything, even though I had my eyes closed. All the hairs in The Mule's nose. The three soldiers who were now standing outside The Shack. One of them was thrusting his hips back and forth like he was having sex. The other two were laughing. A vulture flew by overhead. Then I saw The Mule's index finger slowly push down on the orange plastic trigger of the drill, and the roar of the drill's motor was deafening, and I felt the bit push in and break the skin around my skull.

As you can imagine, this thing with my dreams hasn't always been easy. I've never told anyone about it, not my wife, Mrs. Dugan, and certainly not my daughter Libby, when she was alive, may she rest in peace. And of course I don't always like what I see (the future is not always pleasant), but by far the worst part is the guilt. God, the guilt. Which is to say I always end up feeling like these things happened because I dreamt them first, like the time my next-door neighbor Mr. Gordon's Tricksy turned on him and bit his thumb off. Now it's true I have never liked this Mr. Gordon, given the fact that he got drunk at a neighborhood bar-becue last year and grabbed my wife's right breast in front of everyone and said, "Knock knock," and then she, albeit drunk, smiled in a coy way, and said, "Who's there," which was of course completely humiliating for me, but that's really beside the point, because it's not like I wished Mr. Gordon would get his thumb bit off. But I dreamt it. And then it happened, and so you tell me, how can I not feel a little bit responsible?

All total The Mule put six quarter-inch holes in the back of my head. I was barely conscious. When it was all over, I remember looking up in a steamy haze as The Mule smiled and said, "You are a very stubborn man, Lieutenant Dugan." I was vaguely aware of his putting my ankles in shackles, which were clamped to a stake in the middle of the floor. Then The Mule said, "Per-haps you will die. Perhaps not. But if not, you will be hungry. And maybe when you're hungry, well maybe then you will make the videotape. Good-bye for now, Lieutenant Dugan," and then he slipped out the door.

▪ ▪ ▪

After that things went downhill fast. I was alone with my madness. You've heard it all a hundred times before. The whole POW thing. I went to hell and back in my mind. I gave up hope. My soul was a pink worm stuck through its belly with a hook, and I waited for the Angel of Death to come swimming up out of the darkness and swallow it whole.

That was the first day.

The second day was worse. The second day I started hearing my thirteen-year-old daughter Libby's voice. I knew it was an illusion, but still. I was sitting with my back against the wall, and there were flies buzzing around my head. I heard Libby's voice say, "Lieutenant Jeff Dugan, this is your daughter speaking. Get a hold of yourself. Snap out of it. Yes, it's true, things don't look good, but I'm here to help. You are a Lieutenant in the United States Air Force, and this is war, so keep your wits about you. A little cunning can carry you through."

I realized Libby's voice wasn't inside my head. I looked up and there standing with her back to the door was Libby. Or at least some sort of wavy version of her. She was surrounded by a white, wavy energy. She was well dressed, with fine leather loafers, off-white hose, and a green cashmere turtleneck. Her nose was, as always, small.

I couldn't believe the stupid tricks my mind was playing on me. "You're kidding, right?" I said. "Is this some sort of joke?"

"No, Daddy. It's me. Libby."

I didn't know what to say. "All right then," I said. "Why are you all wavy?"

"Because," she said, and then she told me everything. She said she was dead. She told me about how her Siamese cat, Smoky Joe, had run out in front of a red Chevy and how she had saved Smoky Joe, but was hit and killed in the process. When she was through, I spoke up.

"This is ridiculous. How I am supposed to believe something like that?" I started beating my head with my fist. "Hello? Hello? I know you're in there, brain. I know you're behind this. I expected more from you. Stop it now."

I could tell by the look on Libby's face that she wasn't interested in my cynicism. Her brow was wrinkled, and she was chewing on her bottom lip.

"Look. You aren't real. This is a trick, it's the stress. Please go away. I can't take this."

"Come on. I'm here to help, Daddy," she said. "We've got to get you out of here. Mommy can't lose both of us."

I could feel my temper start to rise. "Yeah, right. Listen, you, whatever the hell you are. You're starting to piss me off."

"Shhhhh. Now that's enough. We don't have time. I have to go now, but I'll be back tomorrow to help you escape," and with that Libby turned and stepped into the wall and passed through it out of sight.


The next morning I woke to someone kicking me in the shins. "Wake up. What are you doing? Sleeping in?" I looked and saw Libby. She was all business. "Okay," she said. "I've been spying in and listening to what they have been saying. Things are getting nuts up there. I think they're planning some sort of attack. The leader seems like a real jerk. You don't want to cross this guy, trust me."

"Ooooh, I'm scared," I said. I pointed to my head. "I've got six holes drilled into my head, and now I've got some wavy figment of my imagination telling me I'm in trouble. Give me a break. What can you tell me about trouble that I don't already know?"

"Daddy, they're going to hang you in the courtyard today. Now. You and some other pilot they captured. They want to make an example of you two, to boost morale before the attack," she said.

"I told you. You're not real." I put my hands over my eyes. "I can't see you."

She kept on. "Okay. So here's what you're going to do. They're coming to get you any minute now. We need to move fast. I'm going to let you out of those shackles. You bend down and act like you're hurt. Then grab the guard's pistol and hit him over the head with it." I suddenly froze. Because it was true, I could hear the guard rustling his keys on the other side of the door. My mouth went dry.

Two seconds later the guard came in and I was lying on the floor, doubled over, pretending to be in pain. "Oh my God, oh my God," I cried.


There was also the time when I was nine. This dream was much fuzzier than the rest, but when I woke in the dead of night I was sweating, and though I couldn't remember what happened, I knew my mom was in danger. And then the next night, right before dinner, I watched as my mother cut a carrot on the cutting board, and wasn't at all surprised when she looked up to tell me to set the table and sliced off her index finger. On the way to the hospital in the ambulance I kept sobbing, "I'm so sorry. I'm so sorry. I'm so sorry."

But the most disturbing dream of all happened two weeks before I had to ship out to Saudi to fight in the Gulf War. This is extremely difficult for me to talk about even now. The dream was swift and simple. I saw my thirteen-year-old daughter Libby run out in the street and get hit and killed by a red Chevy when she tried to shoo her Siamese cat, Smoky Joe, out of the way. Smoky Joe lived. Smoky Joe is short for Smoky Joe the Best Kitty Cat in the World.

And so now you understand. Because each of these events—the thing with Mr. Gordon, the thing with my mom, the thing with Libby—have one thing in common. Each of these things happened in my dream before they happened in reality.

When I burst through the front door of The Shack, the sunlight almost split my eyes open, but then my pupils shrank and I bounded off toward Gracie. To my horror, as I ran over to Gracie, I spotted Captain Jibs hanging by his neck from a rope in the center of the courtyard. A group of soldiers was standing around with their backs to me, jeering at Jibs, throwing rocks at him and spitting on him. When I reached Gracie, I checked behind the seat and all my gear was still there, untouched. I threw on my flak jacket. While I was rifling through my pack I heard a shout and looked up, and there in the doorway of The Shack was the guard rubbing the back of his head. He shouted something in Arabic and pointed at me. The mob around Jibs turned and looked in my direction. There was a moment of silence, and then when they saw me they started screaming and shouting and running.

A siren went off. Dogs started barking.

I took the guard's Beretta 9mm pistol and leapt out of Gracie and ran straight at a parked M60 tank, shooting rounds off left and right, and two men dropped. I ran up the side of the tank and off of it, doing a forward flip, with bullets flying everywhere. I saw a wounded man on the ground reaching for something in his belt. Shot him.

I leapt with my legs wide open and landed on a camel, and shouted, "Huyaaa!," and I rode that camel fast and hard into the middle of the windstorm of bullets and the swarm of Iraqi soldiers. The Mule appeared directly in my path, and the camel skidded to a halt. The Mule said, "This was very stupid, Lieutenant Dugan," and then lobbed a frag grenade. The grenade was in midair when I ripped off my flak jacket and held it in front of the camel's face. The grenade went off and all the shrapnel bounced off my flak jacket. I think that's when the camel knew that I was a compassionate animal. I shouted, "Little help," and the camel rushed forward and head-butted The Mule.

Looking down at The Mule on the ground in that instant, I felt the strangest sensation in my belly button. It felt like my belly button was wiggling around. It was a widening sensation. When I reached down to touch my belly button, I felt a hole in my stomach the size of a silver dollar. My index finger disappeared in the hole, but there was no blood. Just this hole. And then I passed out.


When I came to the camel was galloping over the desert. That was the sound I woke to, the steady *bric-a-brac* of the camel's hooves on the desert floor. My chest kept bouncing against the camel's hump. The sun was just starting to come up, a bloodred squirting over the horizon, as if someone had stuck the sun in a juicer, and I could see the faint silver sliver image of the moon on the other side of the sky. When I looked behind me, the Iraqi camp was a pinpoint on the horizon. "Thank God," I said. "I almost ate it on that one." But as soon as the words were out of my mouth, I realized I had no idea who I was, and I started to panic. I couldn't even remember why I was out here in the desert. I asked myself a question.

When you want to start thinking where do you start?

I didn't know the answer.

My heart jumped up a couple decibels. Still I kept on: riding and pondering my question for as long as I could stand it, but then my brain was suddenly tired from all that thinking, so eventually I figured that until I got my memory back I should keep it simple. The best I could come up with was this: You are a person. You are alive. You are riding a camel.

So I rode through the desert on a camel with no name.

I rode for days and days and days, without food and water. I didn't know where I was going, and hadn't even given it a thought. The sun, that great ball of fire, came up and went down and came up and went down and came up and went down more times than I could count. I watched my haggard shadow do its mindless dance on the desert floor and I watched the horizon.

Once a vicious sandstorm came up in a blur and ate my uniform right off my body. I kept my eyes closed the whole time. The storm came and went. I was completely naked. The camel galloped on like it was in a race against time.

Then one day I looked up and saw ahead of me a palm tree and an oasis of clear blue water. The water shimmered in the heat. My camel had been stumbling throughout the day, and I knew it wasn't long for this world. I considered throwing the camel over my back and carrying him, but I decided against it. I was so thirsty my tongue felt like a balled-up piece of paper in my mouth. I shook my head, and took another look to make sure this wasn't a trick my mind was playing on me. At the sight of the water my camel picked up its pace again, with renewed enthusiasm. It broke into a trot. That camel was amazing. It had a heart of gold. I shouted, "Thata boy! Thata boy!" and the shout came out as a whisper. We were getting closer and closer. I tried to smile, but my lips were exhausted.

And then the camel stumbled, faltered, and came crashing down facefirst, and I was pitched forward, airborne, right to the bank of the oasis. I scraped my knee in the sand. The camel was lying on the ground, floundering like a newborn colt, trying to get back up. It was elegant. It was tragic. I felt like I was witnessing the secret of the universe in the camel's effort. Then it let out a tremendous, "Harrrumpppp," and its soul flew out toward the world beyond.

I named the camel Applejack.

I know you're thinking what's the point in naming something after it's dead, and the answer is: Well, I don't know. But I did it.

The water was a plate of glass. I don't think I ever saw anything so beautiful as that oasis. When I slipped into the water, I could feel the weeks of agony and fear wash off me like a bad cologne. I was clean.

More days passed. This was a time of joy. This was something different than I had ever known. I ate coconuts out of the tree. I didn't understand what was happening, but when I looked at my reflection in the water, I thought, You could be pretty. I let my hair grow out. I put on lipstick that I made from tree sap. I spent most of my time looking down at my reflection. I built a hut out of palm fronds. I made a two-piece bikini bathing suit.

Days days and more days.

Finally I thought: "All right already. It doesn't really matter who I am; everyone needs love. People sound like a pretty good idea." So I set off on foot. I had been walking for centuries. I turned and looked and saw my footprints in the sand as far back as I could see. The entire desert stretched out before me. One day it snowed. Right there in the desert. I know it sounds weird but it did. I was so relieved to be out of the heat that I ran around catching snowflakes on my tongue. I built a snowman named Bert. I shook the snowman's hand and said, "Hi, Bert," and Bert's arm broke off in my grip. Why had Bert's arm broken off but not mine? I laughed out loud because I was so grateful that I still had two arms. I laughed harder than I have ever laughed. I laughed so hard I almost choked on my beard. It seemed to me that the snowman was laughing too, but then Bert said, "Okay. Here's the deal. Your name is Lieutenant Dugan. That's your first clue. People are looking for you. Follow me. I'm going to lead you back to your base."

And that's exactly what Bert did.


Well, it turned out I'd been lost in the desert for six months. And back at Khamis Mushait, I got the POW recovery treatment, which was nice, because I certainly was tired. I slept for three days straight. And it was only afterward, when I woke up and called my wife and she told me that six months before Libby had been killed by a red Chevy, that everything came flooding back into my mind. Because it was then that I remembered how Libby's ghost had appeared and helped me escape from the compound, and it was only then that I truly understood what happened to me out there, what that thing with my belly button was.

My dad didn't want me to die, and so he leapt out of his body and forced me into it, because he wanted me to live. My dad couldn't bear the guilt. That's what that thing with the belly button was. He was leaving his body and pushing me into it. That's how much my dad loved me.

So this is me, Libby. I am a thirteen-year-old girl living inside an air force captain's body. It was the only way. I hide my identity from the rest of the people in my life. I conduct myself as an air force pilot and I report for duty at Holloman AFB and take Gracie up for training runs. It's not so hard to be a captain in the air force, and plus my dad's body remembers how to do everything, so it's a cinch. And like I said, when I'm up there in the cockpit it's like I'm straight out of God's head, a divine thought inside a divine thought bubble, totally invisible. Sometimes I feel bad for my mom, because she doesn't know the truth and I can't tell her. She wouldn't believe me if I did anyway. It would just cause her unnecessary pain.

When I got back to Holloman AFB they awarded me a Silver

Star and bumped my rank up to captain. Then my first day home, my mom drove me out to the cemetery to visit my grave, or should I say the grave where my old body is buried. I forced a tear out for Mom's benefit. The plot was nice. There was an oak tree with a crow in it. On my gravestone it said, *Libby Dugan, Beloved Daughter, Too Good to Be True.* Of course sometimes at night Mom tries to get frisky in bed, but I turn her away. She thinks it's because I'm sad, and she tries to talk to me about it. She says, "I know what's bothering you. But we can get past this. Libby's in heaven now. Life is too beautiful for us to be sad. And we still have each other." But then recently she's started getting mad. She'll start yelling and telling me that the flower inside her is drying up. Well, I always change the subject because it makes me feel funny. Or I'll roll out of bed and go out to the back porch and smoke a cigarette.

Smoky Joe was the only one who knew the truth. He followed me everywhere, rubbing on my shins and jumping into my lap whenever he got the chance. I guess he was grateful to me for saving his life. Sure I was glad to see him too, but he was also causing me massive problems. Because Mom would come home and see Smoky Joe lying on my chest, and say, "That's weird, isn't it, Jeff? I thought Smoky Joe hated you, Jeff. Since you've been home he won't leave you alone." Well, I started to suspect that Mom was on to me. She'd give me these funny looks whenever I tied ribbons to Smoky Joe's tail, or gave him liver treats. Threads were starting to unravel. My story was coming loose. I couldn't sleep at night, and then I'd look down at the foot of the bed and there would be Smoky Joe, staring at me, purring. So it shouldn't come as any surprise that one brisk morning I accidentally backed over Smoky Joe in our driveway with my Ford Bronco.

Other than that it's all good, and sometimes when Mom's still at work I come home early from the base and lock all

the doors to the house and close the curtains and take all
the phones off the hook. Then I go to the back of the closet,
where I keep some things in a trash bag that I don't want anyone to know about. I tape my penis down between my legs and
put on a pair of flowered panties. I put on one of my mom's
dresses and too much lipstick and eyeliner and admire myself in
the big mirror in the living room. On special occasions when I
imagine that I am going to a royal ball, I put on long white
gloves that come up to my elbows. I curtsy, and in my mock
elegant voice I say, "And how do you do? You look so lovely
tonight, dear. Tea? Yes, please. Well, thank you, you are such a
darling."

Which is what I was doing today when Mom came home
early and walked in on me holding our video camera. When I
saw Mom come through the front door, I leapt back out of sight
and dove into the closet. I guess she saw me because she rushed
over and started banging on the door and shouted, "Jeff, I know
you're in there. Come out, Jeff. We need to talk. I know what
you're doing. I've known about this for weeks. There's no need
to hide this anymore, Jeff. I got you on videotape this time. We
need to talk!"

I started getting nervous, with her banging on the door like
that. I was trying to figure a way out of this, where nobody's feel-
ings got hurt, and nobody ended up learning more than he or
she needed to know. My mind was on fire. But at least you know
I'm not crazy. Dr. Barrett, at least now you know. You make sure
you tell this Dr. Hertz as much. You make sure he reads every
single word I've written. And surely now you can understand the
logic of my thesis remark: This world is strange, and to me it is all
very sinister and miraculous.

While I was in the closet I resolved to make a break for it.
I was going to bolt out of there and streak over to my Bronco
and zoom away before my mom could see me. But I didn't know

that my mom knew that that was exactly what I would try to do. I didn't know that my mom had already been in touch with you. I didn't know that when I burst through the closet door and ran out onto the lawn that there would be MPs with tranquilizer guns waiting for me. I didn't know.

# Dear Mr. President

■

October 17, 1991

The Honorable George Bush
President of the United States
The White House
1600 Pennsylvania Avenue
Washington, D.C. 20500

Dear Mr. President,

I remember it like it was yesterday, sir. Yes, the day we met
will always shine bright in my mind, like a beacon as I sail
through the stormy waters of my life. I remember the first
words that I spoke to you, and I hope that you remember them,
too. I was standing in formation, and I said, "Cheddar is better,
sir!" (You had found out that I was from Wisconsin and asked
me if cheddar was better.) And then I half smiled at you, and
you winked, and I knew that we'd made a connection, that you
were someone who understood the real me.

I am sorry. I just want to say I'm sorry for how messy this
letter is because I just now had to wipe some bird poop from it
with a wet Kleenex, and as you can see it smeared a little when
I wiped it. One second I was rehashing our "cheddar is better"
moment, and the next second some bird poop dropped on this

letter. I guess I shouldn't be so surprised, given that I'm having to write this letter to you from up here in the tree. All I can say is imagine what this letter would look like if I didn't have the wet Kleenex.

Anyway, there's not a single person in my family or at my Reserve Unit who doesn't know of our first meeting, and you can rest assured that I will pass our story on to little Jimmy, Jr., just as soon as he is old enough to understand the significance of it. But just in case First Lady Barbara Bush or your son George W., down in Texas—I saw the *60 Minutes* special on you and your family ranch called Western Crusader—haven't yet heard the story of your friend Lance Corporal James Laverne of the United States Marine Corps Reserve, I've enclosed a copy of the picture that was taken of us (it's paper-clipped to the top left corner of this page). That's you wearing the gas mask. I'm not wearing mine because, as you know, the corpsman gave us experimental anti-biological-warfare pills every day so that we didn't have to wear gas masks. Boy, I took more pills over there than I've taken in my entire life. But don't get me wrong, those pills could have saved my life if Saddam actually had used biological warfare. If Saddam's biologically laced Devil Air had ever come and tried to crawl down our mouths and noses and into our lungs, the red pills would have been there to say, "Hey there, Saddam's biologically laced Devil Air, don't even think about it. There's no way you're getting into this American nose and mouth. Nuh-uh. Don't you know that America is the greatest country on earth? You might as well go back to where you came from and try to crawl inside the nose and mouth of the Devil himself, Saddam Hussein. Now scram, Devil Air."

Do you remember the other things you said to me over there in Saudi? Let me refresh your memory. First off, you arrived on one of those fiery days, so hot your brain could cook inside your helmet, like an egg, and some of us had just buried what was left of a couple of ragtag Iraqi border soldiers we'd killed with a mortar attack. What a mess we found when we arrived at that scene, sir! If only you could have seen it. When we jumped down from the Hummer to inspect the damage, it looked like one of those N.E.A. modern-art projects that you see on the news—just a black hole in the ground filled up with charred wood and smoking body parts and blood and hair and sand, and I have to confess that the sight of it made me consider what a long and strange journey life really is.

Anyway, that afternoon I was just hanging around on my rack, writing Mrs. Laverne and little Jimmy, Jr., a letter, telling them about the mortar attack, when some Marine suddenly ducked his head in my hooch and shouted, "The President's here! The President's here! Come on, crazies, the President's here! Fall out in formation, Devil Dogs! Double time! Double time!" I could not believe my ears. I had dreamed of meeting you for so long, sir. I flew out of my hooch with my gear flapping around me and fell into formation so fast it was like my feet had grown wings. I was the first Marine there, that's how fast. And then, in a heartbeat, the rest of my platoon fell into place, and we all stood proudly as your chopper came down, kicking up all that sand and wind so that we had to squint and cough and spit and, eventually, turn our heads. Do you remember how, the first time your chopper tried to land, it came down right on top of our formation, sir? And how we had to scatter at the last second, so that we must have looked like one of those herds of zebras you see on the Discovery Channel, running away from the lion?

Then you hopped off the chopper, and Captain Griffies saluted, and the two of you went into his tent. Now, I don't know what you and Captain Griffies talked about, but it must have been top security because you were in that tent for close to two hours, and of course we all stayed standing at attention, and I think I can speak for all of us, sir, when I say that I had never been more proud to stand at attention, knowing that the President of the United States was hashing out high-priority war strategies not thirty yards away. And when you came out, well, what can I say, that's when you demonstrated your unbelievable leadership skills. You could easily have hopped back on your chopper and sailed away and nobody would have thought anything of it, but that's not what a brilliant leader does, is it, sir? No, sir. I'll tell you what, sir, Sun Tzu could learn a thing or two from you! Because, instead of sailing away, you made your way through the ranks, boosting morale, stopping at each Marine to talk to him, and, boy, did I start to get nervous when you got close to me. My heart was beating so fast! And suddenly there you were, President George Bush, standing right in front of me, Lance Corporal Laverne. In case you were wondering, sir, yes, your voice did sound a little fuzzy, but that's because you had your mask on the whole time. I mean everybody sounds fuzzy when they have a mask on. But not everybody sounds like Darth Vader. No. And that's what you sounded like: Darth Vader with a drawl, only in a cool way.

Anyway, I was standing at attention and you came over and said that thing about cheddar. Then you said, "Relax, son," and you asked me if I knew why I was over here, and I said, yes, sir, I sure as heck did! I said, "We are over here to defend the citizens of the United States of America." And you said I was damn right, and then you leaned over and whispered, "You know what I want you to do, Marine? I want you to go into Kuwait and kick Saddam's butt!" I said, "Yes, sir!" I said it so loud that you jumped back for a second, and your two bodyguards rushed in and stuck their pistols to the back of my head, but, sir, I only said it so loud so that everyone else would know I had just confirmed an order given directly to me by the President of the United States. Maybe I was being a little too proud in front of the other Marines, but we had just made that special connection, and, besides, guess what? Well, you already know what. We went into Kuwait and kicked some major towelhead ass!

I know you're probably busy right now ruling over the Free World, sir, but I just want to give you a few details of that glorious day when we liberated Kuwait—how we rolled out like the cavalry, barreling at top speed through desert lanes that had been swept clear of mines and onto the Main Supply Route for the final approach. Overhead, the Apaches and Cobras were firing missiles at any Iraqi foot soldier or tank or vehicle that made the grave mistake of crossing our path, and there I was, Lance Corporal Laverne, sitting in the high seat of our Hummer, bouncing around as we sailed over the dunes. We were all wearing our War Grimace, with our weapons ready, because who knew what lay ahead, and, off in the distance, we could see the first oil wells burst into billows of fire and black smoke. I felt for a moment as if this were truly World War III, or, more precisely, Hell, and here we were, endowed by God Almighty—Manifest Destiny come back to the Holy Land to cast out the Prince of Darkness himself.

As we approached Kuwait, we kept getting spot radio reports about a firefight at the airport, and my squad was dispatched to provide support. In our three Hummers, we smashed through the wire fence that surrounded the airport and stormed down the runway, and that's when we heard another report, this one about a sniper on the roof of the airport, so Private Breeks and I dumped our Hummer and sprinted through the chaos and into the main building. The door to the roof was locked, so I C-4'ed it open, but what we saw when we stepped through the smoke onto the roof took us by surprise, sir. Breeks said, "That's no sniper. That poor thing's going to get hurt." And he was right, because all there was on the gravel roof was a dog, a beagle, with a stick in its mouth. Then just as Breeks darted over to the dog, I remembered those stories about the Vietcong kids who ran up to G.I.s with lit sticks of dynamite in their butts, and I shouted, "Breeks! No! No, Breeks!" But Breeks scooped up the beagle and turned to me with a grin on his face, and I saw that the stick in the beagle's mouth was just a stick, and I breathed a sigh of relief. And that's when we heard a clatter, and a grenade bounced across the roof and came to rest against Breeks's boot. Breeks, still grinning, dropped the dog and was blown straight up into the air. You have to understand that this all happened really fast, sir. In a couple of seconds, really. Breeks's body twisted in what looked to be a perfect triple gainer, ripped in half at the waist, and landed in pieces on the gravel roof. Private Breeks had been torn in two like a movie ticket.

Well, I charged over to the far corner of the roof, where the grenade had come from, and there was this Iraqi soldier crouched behind a plaid suitcase, with half of his bushy-haired head peeking over the top of it. I whipped out my Beretta and shouted, "Hold it right there!" and that's when I thought I heard Breeks calling out for help: "I'm broken, Laverne! Oh, Christ, I'm broken, Laverne!" The Iraqi soldier was suddenly up and inching sideways along the edge of the roof with his hands over his head, and I could feel the situation starting to get away from me. I shouted over my shoulder, "Breeks? Breeks? Is that you?" But when I glanced back I saw that what I'd thought was Breeks was just the stupid dog, barking its head off, "Ruff! Ruff!" and then the Iraqi bolted and dived through the door. Sir, I didn't know what to do. I felt dizzy, and my mind went numb. For a long moment, my head seemed to be shot through with a hot white light, and then, as if my body were acting without me, I lunged at the dog, snatched it up by its hind leg, and bashed its head against the ground. I did this over and over and over and over. Then I unsheathed my K-bar and went to work.

A few minutes later, someone came up behind me and said, "What the hell is that, Marine?" I could tell by the voice that it was Sergeant Muller. So I spun around with what was left of the dog in my hands, and gasped, "I just killed this enemy here, Sarge!" Muller looked around for a second, and then he said, "No, not that, Laverne, you idiot, I'm talking about that," and he pointed at my stomach. I looked down and said, "I don't know what you're talking about, Sarge." Then Sergeant Muller said, "There, Marine. Right there. Lift your shirt right now, Marine. Laverne, if you don't lift your shirt, I'm going to kick your ass right here in the middle of this war! Is that what you want? Do you want me to kick your ass right here in the middle of this war?" So I lifted my shirt, because it was common knowledge in my unit that Muller was crazy and that people who got on Muller's bad side had a nasty habit of ending up in the hospital for weird stuff, like pulling the pin on a grenade and then falling on it or waking up in the middle of the night choking on an M.R.E. that they didn't remember opening.

The other guys from 1st Platoon had arrived now, and the instant I lifted my shirt I heard someone say, "Holy shit!" Then someone else said, "Goddamn, what the hell is that?" And they all just started laughing. This was some really deep belly laughing. I mean I have never heard people laugh as hard as those guys were laughing. They were laughing so hard that I forgot all about Breeks and the enemy I'd just killed and the firefight that was still going on down on the runway, and I couldn't help smiling a little, because this was the kind of laughter that makes you want to join in. Then we were all laughing together. I was laughing so hard I felt dizzy again, as if all the air in my head were lifting my body up off the ground like a balloon.

But when I glanced down I immediately stopped laughing. Because there, on my second rib up on my left side, was a perfectly shaped human ear. And suddenly I couldn't hear anything, not the deep belly laughing or the rounds going off. Not even my own breathing. All of Kuwait had gone silent. Whole years seemed to pass as I stared at the ear on my second rib up on my left side, growing right out of my skin. It was technically my ear, I guess. My third ear. Looking down at that ear, I felt a wave of nausea wash over me. And that's when Sergeant Muller said, "Jesus, you've got problems, Laverne. I'll tell you what. You stay the fuck away from me, Laverne. I swear to God, Laverne, you come near me, and it will be the last fucking thing you ever do. You hear me?" And then he turned to his guys and said, "Let's get the hell out of here."

Well, sir, I stayed up on the roof for the next two hours, as the sky slowly turned black with the smoke from the burning wells. But by then I wasn't paying attention anymore, because for all that time I never once took my eyes off that ear. I studied the ear. I touched the ear. I even tried to lick the ear. And then, when I finally heard the city-wide Chemical Alert go off, I shook my head, dropped my shirt, yanked my MOPP Level 4 gear out of my ruck, and scrambled into it. (In case you don't know, sir, MOPP 4 gear consists of a heavy coat and pants, rubber gloves, rubber boots, and gas mask—thus the nickname Body Condom.) And as I hightailed it off the roof and caught up with the Marines from my squad, with whom I would go on to kill four more Iraqi soldiers, the only thing I knew for sure, right there in the middle of that war, was that the difference between this new third ear of mine and the two ears on my head was that this one didn't have a hole in it. Yes, sir, this third ear of mine was deaf.

I was over in Saudi for another seven months after the

cease-fire, pulling different duties, running a checkpoint on a
highway between Baghdad and Basra, patrolling the DMZ near
Umm Qasr, breaking down tent cities in places whose names I
can't remember, and for those seven months I tried not to think
about the ear. I forced myself to forget about it. Which was
easy, because I just didn't look at it again. Out of sight, out of
mind, is what I was thinking. And I'll tell you what, sir, it
worked. I mean, how many times do you need to look at your
second rib up on your left side anyway? After a while, I just
forgot about that ear. And if by some strange chance I
happened to touch it with the inside of my left arm while I was
toting my M-16, or if I snagged a sheet on it while I was tossing
and turning in the rack, or if I accidentally ran my hand over it
when I was soaping up in the shower, well, I would tell myself
that it was a dream. I'd say, "Lance Corporal Laverne, you are
dreaming. You think you just touched an ear growing on your
second rib up on your left side, but you did not, because you
are dreaming. Dreams are stupid, and they don't mean a thing."
Then I would pretend to wake up. No matter where I was, I
would stretch and yawn and scratch my head. And, in this way,
the ear ceased to exist, sir.

The ear certainly didn't exist when I arrived back in
Madison, on that first day, when my unit was ushered straight
to the WE'RE-GLAD-YOU'RE-HOME-NOW-FIND-YOUR-
WOMAN (AND-IF-YOU'RE-GAY-WE-DON'T-WANT-TO-
KNOW-ABOUT-IT) ticker-tape parade that was being thrown
downtown. And, as I stood at the center of the Got Oil? float
in my dress blues surrounded by strippers with red, white, and
blue streamers hanging from their nipples, I didn't once think
about the ear. As the sounds of the marching band and my
fellow Americans' cheers filled my head, all I could think
about was how happy I was to be home. I was grateful to be
able to buy a Snickers bar, to be able to do the little things
that are my God-given right as an American to do. I waved like

crazy when I saw Mrs. Laverne in her red dress. She had
Jimmy, Jr., on her shoulders, and he was waving a tiny
American flag and clutching a red balloon. It was one of those
sunny, cool Madison days, so beautiful that you feel blessed,
and this was one of the greatest moments of my adult life—
out among the people of my hometown, feeling all that love.
Because when it's all said and done, what it boils down to, sir,
is love. Isn't that right?

But after I got home from the parade that night, and kissed
little Jimmy, Jr., on the head as he was sleeping, and went into
the bedroom, Mrs. Laverne took my shirt off and saw the ear
and threw up and fainted. And that's when I thought about the
ear again, sir, and I knew I wasn't dreaming anymore. The ear
was real. Yes, sir, as Mrs. Laverne lay there twitching in her own
vomit, I looked straight at my second rib up on my left side in
the full-length mirror and saw that that ear had now officially
made its way into reality.

We went to the V.A. hospital a couple of days later, and Dr.
Dunard told me what I had suspected all along: there was
nothing wrong with me. He said that the ear was benign, and
that there was no connection between it and my service over in
Saudi Arabia. He also said that I was probably suffering from
post-traumatic stress syndrome and that he wanted to put
me on Prozac. When Mrs. Laverne heard this she got very
excited, as women sometimes do, and she started throwing
chairs and files around Dr. Dunard's office, screaming, "If
there's nothing wrong with him, then what the hell is that?
What the hell is that thing? Are you telling me that my
husband is a freak? My husband went to war in the Persian
Gulf and he didn't have this ear on his stomach, and now he's
back from the war and he has this ear on his stomach, and
you're telling me there's nothing wrong with him?" As I said,
sir, she was pretty excited. And I started getting excited,

too, what with everything she was saying, and I didn't know what to do with this excitement, sir. I was getting all hopped up and jittery. But eventually Dr. Dunard gave her a shot of something and got her calmed down, and we drove home in silence.

That night, the house was very quiet, except when I heard Mrs. Laverne sobbing in the bathroom and later when I woke up in the middle of the night and Mrs. Laverne was screaming at me. She was saying, "Saddam used biological warfare, that's why you got that third ear. I saw it on CNN! You stupid jarhead freak! The government doesn't give a damn about you. Your so-called good friend George Bush doesn't give a damn about you. You're nothing but a jarhead to him! I want you to call a lawyer first thing tomorrow, and we're going to take this to the Supreme Court!" Well, sir, I knew that she was in a state, what with all the excitement of my coming back home. That can be hard on the wives of soldiers, and I didn't want to rile her up any more than she already was, so I said, "Sure, hon, I promise I'll get on the horn just as soon as I finish building that tree house for Jimmy, Jr." But, of course, I never did make the call.

Instead, I built Jimmy the best damn tree house you can imagine. I installed a rope ladder that he could raise up and drop down. I built a little deck with a telescope on it and painted it with Thompson's WaterSeal. I built a kitchenette with a sink and a microwave oven. I put in a makeshift toilet, and I hooked up a power generator so there was electricity. And I put a TV and a shortwave radio up there. I wanted nothing but the best for Jimmy, Jr., plus the work kept my mind off things.

The truth is, I didn't really care about the ear, and I was sad that Mrs. Laverne couldn't love me for who I was. Besides, I was starting to get highly pissed at her for all the trouble she was causing. What's one ear more or less, anyway, sir? It's not like it was causing me any pain. I mean, sure, if I accidentally touched it, grazed it or whatever, it felt like a burning-hot coal was searing through my skin until I put an ice cube on it, but other than that it was fine. Don't get me wrong. If I had my choice, I would rather the ear weren't there, but it wasn't a big deal. What I like to do is think of the ear as a flower. A sunflower that has bloomed on my body and is growing. People come home from war a lot worse off than I did—missing arms and legs and teeth and eyes. People come home dead. In fact, if you think about it, I gained something, as opposed to losing something. That makes me a winner is what I kept trying to tell Mrs. Laverne.

Then about a week ago, for no reason that I could tell, I woke up in the middle of the night. And I happened to glance over at Mrs. Laverne lying there asleep with her head buried in the pillow, and I saw a tiny shining thing buried in the thick black hair on the back of her head. A glint of something, caught in the moonlight. I was half asleep, and in a distant part of my mind I was thinking, What the heck is that? But I was drowsy, and before I knew it I'd closed my eyes and drifted back off into never-never land. The next night the same thing happened. I woke up, and, for no reason at all, I rolled over, and there was this shiny thing on Mrs. Laverne's head. I sure wish I had gone back to sleep again, which is what I should have done, because of how completely exhausted I was. But, instead, I reached over and parted Mrs. Laverne's hair to get a better look.

It took me a second to realize what the shiny thing was. It was a tooth. A perfect shiny white tooth. One of many teeth, two rows of teeth, to be exact, set inside an honest-to-God mouth, with lips and everything else that comes with a mouth. I reached out and touched its upper lip. It was soft, sir, really soft. This was a real mouth, on the back of Mrs. Laverne's head. A tongue darted out and licked the spot on the lip I had just

touched. Then the mouth said, "Hi, Laverne." I froze. The
mouth said, "Hey, buddy. What's happening? What do you
think? Not too shabby, huh?" The mouth had a high-pitched
squeaky man's voice, and I certainly didn't like the tone it was
taking with me. So I asked it what the hell it was doing on the
back of my wife's head, and who the hell did it think it was
talking to. And the mouth said, "I am talking to you, Laverne.
What—are you kidding me? Come on. You're a real class act,
Laverne. Like you don't know who you are, huh? Hi, my name's
Laverne, and I don't know who I am! Hey, Laverne, what do
you think Mrs. Laverne is going to do when she finds me on the
back of her head, huh? Do you think she's going to brush these
teeth of mine, Laverne? Because I'll tell you what, Laverne,
I am definitely into oral hygiene. When you've got a set of
pearlies as beautiful as mine, you want to do everything you
can to keep them up." Then the mouth curled its lips back and
bared what I have to admit was a beautiful set of teeth. "Not
too shabby, huh?"

I was starting to get pissed, and I told the mouth so, and I
said that it would be in its best interest to answer my first
question in regards to what the hell did it think it was doing on
the back of my wife's head. And the mouth said, "Hey, cool your
jets, Laverne. Calm down. I'm here because of you. I'm here
because you went over to Saudi and fought in the war, Laverne.
What am I missing here? Come on. How could you not know
this? You'd better wake up, Laverne. Get a grip." And that's
when I knew that this new mouth on the back of Mrs. Laverne's
head was a goddamn big-time liar, and I told him as much.
Then the mouth said, "Laveeeeerne. Now, it doesn't look like
my pants are on fire, does it, Laverne? No, I don't think my
pants are on fire. I am not lying, old friend." Well, what could I
do, sir? I mean, what would you have done if you woke up in
the middle of the night and First Lady Barbara Bush had a

mouth on the back of her head? One thing was for sure: I couldn't do what I wanted to do, which was punch that mouth in the mouth, because that would almost be like punching Mrs. Laverne. Instead, I put a big strip of duct tape over the mouth, and went back to sleep.

The next morning, everything went haywire. I woke up and saw Mrs. Laverne standing in front of the full-length mirror, trying to pull something off her face with her hands. She was jerking this way and that, and for a second it seemed like she was a mime giving a performance that involved trying to pull her face off her head. Then my vision came into better focus and I understood: in my drowsy state the night before, I must have accidentally taped her normal mouth shut.

Mrs. Laverne whirled and faced me, and when I saw the look in her eyes, for a split second, I thought just maybe it was a good thing that her mouth was taped shut, given the things she would likely have said to me at that moment. I didn't have long to consider this though, because then she hurled a bar of Dove and tagged me square in the head, knocking me back on the bed. I was seeing blue stars. And, through the blue stars, I saw Mrs. Laverne rapidly advancing with a curling iron raised over her head. And I was thinking that this was definitely not the way I wanted to die, when little Jimmy, Jr., came walking into the room, rubbing his eyes, with his blanket draped around him, and said, "Daddy? Daddy? What's going on?" And we, Mrs. Laverne and I, both stopped and turned to look at our little boy, and I said, "Oh, my God!" Because there, in plain sight, was little Jimmy, Jr., with what was clearly his normal face except for one thing: his nose was gone. His face was flat as a pancake. And there were no little nostril holes. My little Jimmy, Jr., didn't have a nose.

Please, sir, whatever you do, don't take this the wrong way. Even as I watched Mrs. Laverne carry her suitcase and Jimmy,

Jr., out the door I maintained my position, which, of course, is
your position: Saddam Hussein did not use biological warfare in
Saudi Arabia. If there's one thing I hate, it's a whiner. I hate all
these so-called Desert Storm veterans with headaches and hair
falling out who go around saying that they have something
called Gulf War Syndrome. Like Corporal Hale, who lives
down the street. He can't walk. He has to sit on a skateboard
when he wants to go somewhere, and he comes over to my
house with pus spots on his face and wants to blame the United
States government. The other day he tried to get me to sign a
petition, because a couple of weeks ago I made the mistake of
getting drunk with him and showing him the ear. Hale looked
up at me and said, "Come on, Laverne. Don't be so gung-ho.
We're all in this together. You deserve better than this. Think of
little Jimmy, Jr." At the time, I was up here in Jimmy, Jr.'s tree
house (where I have temporarily taken up residence), and Hale
was down in my backyard. He was waving a piece of paper over
his head, and I could make out the words YOU WANTED OIL
AND WE GOT IT FOR YOU, NOW HELP US! typed at the top of it.
So I calmly pointed my Beretta down at him and said, "You
would do well not to mention my son's name again, Hale. In
fact, you would do well not ever to think about my son again,
Hale."

And that's when the idea about flying kicked in. As Hale
wheeled himself out of the backyard and down the driveway, I
leaned out to watch, lost my balance, and fell to the ground. I
landed on my back. For several minutes, I thought I was
paralyzed, because I couldn't move my limbs. Then I must have
blacked out. When I woke up, the stars were strewn across the
night sky, and a copy of Hale's petition was taped to my chest.
That was four days ago. Eventually, I got back up here, and I
haven't been back down since. My back is killing me, but it
hurts less when I stay hunched over. That's how I'm sitting now,

hunched over. And, with all these birds around, a thought occurred to me: Maybe the pain in my back wasn't from the fall but was some sort of growing pains for wings that were about to sprout on my back. Like when a tooth hurts before it comes in. I figure that's not too much to ask for. I figure if you can get an ear or a mouth, then it's possible to get a set of wings. And, of course, if I had wings I could fly out to my mother-in-law's house in Seattle, and I know that if Mrs. Laverne looked up in the sky and saw me flying with my new wings, she would get over the ear and mouth and nose thing. Who could turn down a man with wings? So I've been checking for them every morning, but they haven't come in yet, and I feel like I'm running out of time.

That's why I was wondering if you could do an old friend a favor and write Mrs. Laverne a short note to tell her that she should come home with Jimmy, Jr., so that we can be a family again. I know we have some problems, but they're nothing that our love can't overcome. Could you tell her that you are proud of me and that I served my country honorably? Could you tell her that I said she should come back so we can start the healing? I'm afraid she just won't listen to me anymore, sir. She won't even talk to me. The last time I called over there, she put the mouth on the phone and the mouth said, "Jesus, don't you ever give up, Laverne? Don't you think we know it's you that keeps calling in the middle of the night? Can't you take a hint, Laverne?" and that's when I hung up. Because I definitely wasn't going to sit there and take that from that lying son of a bitch.

I sure would appreciate you writing that letter, sir. Please send it to 381 Bengal Street, Seattle, WA 98122, which is my mother-in-law's address. Then maybe I could start to get my life back. I mean if a man doesn't have his family, what does he have? I miss carrying Jimmy, Jr., around on my shoulders and playing Dinosaur, and the only company I have is the birds up here in the tree. Winter is coming on, and the leaves are falling off. Soon, even the birds will be gone. I know you'll understand, sir. And I know Mrs. Laverne will listen to you. Please give my best to First Lady Barbara Bush, George W., and Jeb. Yes, sir. Tell them I said hi and that I think of them often. And, as always, it is an extreme honor to serve under you, sir.

SEMPER FIDELIS,
Lance Corporal James Laverne

# The American
# Green Machine

■

Good morning, CLARENCE T. FORDHAM, please do not be alarmed, because I can imagine what you are contemplating right now as you struggle to attain consciousness and the answer is no, this is not a confidential message from God that has been precision-guided into your head, but it is certainly the next best thing, because I am without question a card-carrying member of God's most celebrated band of brothers and sisters: the United States Marine Corps. CLARENCE T. FORDHAM, my name is Recruiter Staff Sergeant Hartigan of the United States Marine Corps, and our records indicate that this May you will be graduating from LYNDON BAINES JOHNSON HIGH SCHOOL (go BRAHMAS), and so I wanted to take this opportunity to personally congratulate you on your forthcoming graduation and to discuss the possibility of an exhilarating and rewarding career in my beloved corps.

But first I would like to ask you one simple question. CLARENCE T. FORDHAM, can you tell me what you accomplished yesterday? Because it is extremely important to me that you know that in the course of performing my duties yesterday as a staff sergeant in the United States Marine Corps I accomplished these things:

- Went scuba diving in the Atlantic Ocean, where I not only executed a top-priority mission, but also saw a wide array of fascinating and ecologically significant aquatic life

- Employed incredibly dangerous underwater demolitions to blow a hole in the ocean floor the size of an SUV

- Saved a young man's life

CLARENCE T. FORDHAM, if you are processing this text in black print on what appears to be a white/off-white background, then that means you have received your first BRAIN-MAIL®, which is to say that yesterday, I, Recruiter Staff Sergeant Hartigan, issued a direct order and then last night a reconnaissance Marine entered your residence by any means necessary and, with the aid of a scalpel and scissors and a piece of black thread, installed the newest 720-Wireless Extended Range Data Link (WERDL) in your head while you were asleep. Now obviously we would not have elected to install the WERDL in your head had we not received from you the no-postage-necessary American Citizen Poll Postcard with Democratic Multiple Choice Question (ACPPDMCQ), on which you astutely checked answer C. Saddam Hussein + weapons of mass destruction = evil.

How this works is with the simple flip of a switch here at our office, the WERDL manifests an artificial computer screen up on the inside rear plate of your skull, thereby prompting your mind's eye to metabolize the information on this screen through a response method innate to the modern central nervous system, known as Picking Fruit. Unfortunately, at this time, we only possess the admittedly limited capacity to receive messages with our brains and not to compose and send out, but each day our elite panel of bioresearchers and computer programmers take significant steps toward making this a reality, because BRAIN-MAIL® is a vital component of America's exclusive 900 SLAM weapon system.

CLARENCE T. FORDHAM, now that you have been informed as to how it is that you are receiving this message inside your head, and what our motivation is in contacting you, I am under obligation by law to inform you that should you continue to process beyond this paragraph, this act will imply your consent to a) allow the WERDL to remain in your head even if you decide not to enlist in the United States Marine Corps, and b) allow a government-sponsored surgeon to enter your residence while you are asleep and through a simple pain-free procedure erase any memory you might have of the WERDL's presence in your head. However, if you do not want to process this message further and subsequently discover how you can shape your life into a winning success story beyond your wildest dreams, and if instead you want to abort this exchange, please carefully peel the Military Vision Restraints (MVR) from your eyes and pick up a phone immediately and dial 1-800-YES-JOIN, and you will speak with one of our representatives who can deactivate your WERDL with the flip of a switch.[1]

Congratulations, CLARENCE T. FORDHAM, you have now successfully overcome the first Human Strategy Obstacle (HSO) toward metamorphizing into not only a member of the most elite fighting force in the history of the world, but an invincible emblem of justice and peace and the American way. Let me be the first to say that I am proud to call you my brother, and as such I would like to ask you one last simple question: How many people who have a PROSTHETIC LEG can emphatically declare that they are an invincible emblem of justice and peace and the American way? Yes, that is correct, CLARENCE T. FORDHAM, we are fully cognizant of the fact that you have a PROSTHETIC LEG, and further, that it was your intention to conceal your condition from us because you surmised said knowledge would terminate the possibility of membership in our elite fraternity. However, CLARENCE T. FORDHAM, we are also cognizant of the fact that your condition has endowed you with an incomprehensible amount of physical and mental anguish, because before we consider offering membership to an individual, we disseminate representatives into the world to solicit firsthand testimonials and assessments regarding the individual in question from friends, family members, and peers. We meticulously compile a United States Marine Corps Personnel Report. Below you will find an excerpt from your very own United States Marine Corps Personnel Report:

## USMC PERSONNEL REPORT ON CLARENCE T. FORDHAM[2]

1. MARTIN FITCH: I haven't ever talked to Clarence but I know who he is and I know he knows who I am, because our last names start with *F* so we've always been in the same homeroom. This year he's in my Calculus II class, and I've always wanted to be nice to him, but since he has that fake leg I never know what the right thing to do is because if I act friendly to him I don't want him to think I feel sorry for him, but on the flip side I don't want him to think I don't care either, so what I do is ignore him, and that way he knows I really do care. Last month Clarence hobbled into class and his eyes were bloodshot and it looked like he'd been crying. He kept snuffling through class, and at first I think we all tried to ignore it out of a sense of courtesy, even the teacher, Mrs. Phillips, who was busy running through quadratic equations at the blackboard, but then the snuffling got louder, so finally Mrs. Phillips sidled over to his desk and bent down and whispered something in his ear,

and then he whispered something back and busted out sobbing. Then he grabbed his stuff and raced out the door. Well, I only found out what happened the next day. It turns out some of the jocks in gym class had pinned him down in the locker room and stolen his fake leg while singing "O Christmas Tree." Then the jocks tied the leg to the flag in front of our school, so when the bell rang after sixth period everyone poured out the front doors and there was Clarence's naked leg dangling from the top of the flagpole.

2. KRISTEN WEMBERLY: Isn't that the guy who was born in a test tube? Didn't the test tube explode when they tried to pull him out of it?

3. GENE KASPER: Clarence is "different," I knew that right off. When I first fell in love with Donna, I thought she was too good to be true, I mean yeah, of course she'd been married before, and that meant she'd already done all the kinky, keep-the-marriage-spicy stuff with some other guy, the backdoor stuff and the pretend-rape-by-candlelight stuff, but I didn't care, because when you're a second husband like me, there's just some things you don't talk about if you want to be able to sleep at night. But when we were dating I kept waiting for the catch, because Donna was so perfect and everything, and I remember how relieved I was the first time I saw her bare feet and she didn't have four toes. But then one night she brought me home and the bottom dropped out. I saw Clarence sitting on the couch and he wasn't wearing his leg, and Donna said, "Gene, meet my son Clarence." And then Clarence got up and hopped over to me, and I thought, Oh shit. Of course I never let on, I mean it's not Clarence's fault that he was born that way. Plus I loved Donna, so the very next week I popped the question. Clarence has a disability, and sure, I'd be lying if I

didn't say that I'd love to have a son who I could cheer for from the stands. But you have to accept people for who they are, right?

CLARENCE T. FORDHAM, all of the above testimonials are supreme examples of acute and misdirected idiocy, because your PROSTHETIC LEG is a sign of what you have always secretly known: you were deposited on the face of this earth to do something spectacular and unforgettable, because when you lie in bed at night and look into the future and envision yourself showing the world how valuable you truly are, well, this is the truth. And while we are on the slippery subject of truth, I feel compelled to confess that when I claimed to have saved a young man's life yesterday I was lying, because the young man's life I was referring to having saved was yours, CLARENCE T. FORDHAM, and we both know that that is happening right now, today, not yesterday.

So in order for you to comprehend what I am alluding to, I want you to carefully peel the MVRs from your eyes, but please keep processing this message after you peel the MVRs from your eyes, and be sure to lift the blankets back so your entire body is visible. Now do you see what I am talking about, CLARENCE T. FORDHAM? Can you see the miracle that I am talking about, CLARENCE T. FORDHAM? God, I wish I was there to see the look on your face, CLARENCE T. FORDHAM.

Because what you are looking at, Devil Dog, is a GO-DURA-LIFE-LEG®, which is yet another brilliant innovation manufactured by Syntechillate, LLC, a little known Bermuda-based subsidiary of the United States Marine Corps. Now, clearly this GO-DURA-LIFE-LEG® appears in every capacity to be an actual human leg, right down to the client-customized pigmentation and color-coordinated leg hair, but the truth is this GO-DURA-LIFE-LEG® will radically out-perform an actual human leg, because the artificial muscles have been enhanced through a cutting-edge process known as robo-gene-modification, which is to say that you will never even have to exercise this leg as it is designed to achieve optimal performance no matter how small or large the task. So go ahead, give it a test run, take that new GO-DURA-LIFE-LEG® of yours for a jog around the block. Go be the miracle that you are now with your new GO-DURA-LIFE-LEG®. Go kick a perfect field goal from the opposite end zone, and, while you are at it, do us both a favor and go kick down KRISTEN WEMBERLY'S door and declare that you are a United States Marine and watch her melt in your hands.

But before you do any of these things, CLARENCE T. FORDHAM, I want you to sprint down here to see me at the Marine Corps Recruitment Center (MCRC) on Congress Avenue and sign some documents and take a videotaped sworn oath stating that you will consentually accompany me to the Military Enlistment Processing Station (MEPS) one week from today. I want you to sprint down here and burst through the doors and I will be standing here waiting with the papers all drawn up, CLARENCE T. FORDHAM, and you will be in and out of my office in less than an hour and then you will be free to walk around on your new GO-DURA-LIFE-LEG®, knowing in your heart that you did the right thing for yourself and for your country today. So what do you say, CLARENCE T. FORDHAM? That is truly my last and final question. What do you say?

---

1. I should warn you, though, this welcome gesture on the part of the corps is a onetime offer, so please make your choice carefully but quickly, because time is of the essence and after a predetermined amount of time expires without our receiving a phone call from you, we will have no choice but to assume that you have elected to read further.°

° Due to legal constraints, we are not allowed to indicate exactly how much time you have left.

2. The United States Marine Corps is an equal opportunity employer.

# General Schwarzkopf
# Looks Back at
# His Humble Beginning

■

I thought I was dead, but really I'd just been born, pushed out into the bright light by the big powerful walls of my mom's vagina. I was one of those "blue babies," which meant that I had to live in a glass case for the first two months of my life. Every day my parents would come to the hospital and look down at me with their faces full of hope, and we'd talk back and forth, me by waving my arms around and wiggling my little fingers, and them by pointing and smiling at me. I kept telling them things couldn't go on like this forever, and that I wanted to be buried pronto. I kept telling them don't come back until you bring a hearse. I'd say, "Let's get this show on the road."

That was back when my heart was the size of a raisin. You could have taken my heart out and put it in a box of raisins and nobody would know the difference. You could have packed the box of raisins in your kid's lunch bag and nobody would know the difference. And your kid could have thrown my heart at some girl he had a crush on and accidentally put her eye out with it, so that the girl grew up and got a black belt in karate, so that there was a tiny bit less love in the world than there should have been because there was a lonely one-eyed karate master woman roaming the streets at night, and nobody would know the difference.

# Sneak and Peek
# Outside Baghdad

■

When dawn broke, I spotted a couple of gigantic pigs snoozing thirty feet or so away in the dust, next to an abandoned train track that ran alongside the highway. Bedouins in cloaks suddenly appeared toting primitive wood rakes and hoes, hitting the fields, while mongrel dogs scampered around, yapping their ancient, unintelligible song, and furtive women dragged their children by the hand as if by a leash. This was a vibrant community, but Intel had assured us there'd be no one here. Fucking Intelligence.

I turned and was startled by an Arab kid standing stock-still maybe ten feet away in the wheat with his eyes glued to me. He must have been about thirteen, with a white turban piled high on his head like a reverse snowcone.

I put a threatening finger to my lips.

The kid spoke up with a broken Arabian accent. "Yu be kwiet yu own self, beetch. Whade fuck. Allyu git de hell out now. Yu trespasseen. Thees privut property."

We poured out out of the Hide Site with our rifles and surrounded the kid, and Thrash stuck the tip of his 9mm to the kid's forehead. In broad daylight, with civilians everywhere. Fucking Intelligence.

The kid seemed oblivious to Thrash. "Oly sheet. Whos de weetback?" he said, pointing at Jesus.

"Stay cool," Rachel said. "Easy, T. He's just a kid."

Jesus went, "Yeah, he's just repeating something he's heard."

"Sheet," said the Arab kid. "I know yu weetbacks swim into America an suck de tit uf tax-payin citisens. Don't tell me wut the fuk I no, azzhol."

Rachel crouched down and spoke gently to the boy, slowing her speech. "H-o-w d-o y-o-u s-p-e-a-k E-n-g-l-i-s-h s-o w-e-l-l?" What were we now, the Peace Corps?

I barked at Rachel: "Why don't you try to *control* this situation?"

Keeping her eyes on the kid, she said, "Yeah, right, just like you did with Sandra. Why don't you give me a lesson in *control,* Frank." Rachel's potshot was a swift kick in the nuts, and my mind, suddenly slick with the pain of memory, shot out into the wide, pitiless sky above.


Sandra, my ex-fiancée, was a flirty night-shift waitress at May-belle's on the outskirts of Fayetteville when I met her, and I ordered the Country Breakfast. Sandra was also, I found out later, a nymphomaniac, or, excuse me, I should say an R.N., that was her little joke: a Recovering Nymphomaniac. By the time I found out about Sandra's condition she'd already moved in. I woke up one night and she was crying big silent tears at the ceiling, and when I asked her what's wrong, she said she'd never been this happy and she was scared she was going to mess it up. That's when she told me about her sexual impulses and her sordid past, including her stepfather, Ralph, a cheerful country-club golf pro in Georgia who used to stick golf balls up in her because he said it helped his game. I said, Go see a psychologist, I'm here for you. The psychologist she ended up with was a mustached man named Kevin, a Cornell graduate who specialized in something called poststructural psychology. Kevin suggested that Sandra start dancing at Brad's Wet & Wild Gurls as a method of boosting her self-esteem. He emphasized the word *method.* I have to admit I wasn't wild about the idea, but I loved Sandra and I was willing to do whatever it took to start the healing.

The Arab kid got real nasty. He demanded that Rachel stick a veil over her face pronto, and Rachel said she didn't believe in Allah but that she very much respected the kid's belief system.

The Arab kid said, "No Allah. Yu butt ugly."

Thrash went, "Watch your suckhole," and drilled the Arab kid in the shin. The kid crumpled, and then Thrash, leaning down with the 9mm against the kid's temple, started to squeeze the trigger.

The kid blurted out, "Coca-Cola Culture Vulture Exchange Program." He said he did his seventh and eighth grades in Des Moines, Iowa. "That's how cum I speek E-n-g-l-i-s-h s-o w-e-e-l-l." He winced and got to his feet and pointed with conviction at Jesus. "I no ask agin. Whut's thees fuckin spick doin on mah dad's fahm?"

I could not take any more. I shoved Thrash out of the way and got right up in that Arab kid's face and growled, "I think the word you're looking for is Mexican American."

I do not like to hurt people, but I cannot tolerate a bigot. One of the things I love about the army is that it is color blind. Before the army, back at my high school, St. Albans in D.C., I went through some "adjustment problems," and I am sure not proud of this but I accidentally fell in with a couple of friendly white supremacists from my trigonometry class.

Today, though, some of my best friends are African American and Mexican American and Native American. That is what the army taught me, and these days I am racked with personal guilt for the way America has treated minorities, and when the ATM machine asks if I want instructions in English or Spanish, I pick

Spanish, even though I do not understand a lick of it. Just my little way of saying yes to diversity. So when I hear a racist shooting off his mouth, something inside of me boils over and I go ballistic: I become an animal.

That is how I explain what happened next, with that Arab kid who kept using the word spick. It was that Arab kid using the S-word that made me grab his turban and sling him facefirst in the dirt.

There was a loud snort, and I glanced back and spotted one of those gigantic pigs lumbering to its feet and starting to trot in our direction. Jesus chuckled, and said, "Whoa, Frank. Looks like you pissed somebody off."

I turned to Jesus with a grin.

That pig smashed into the side of my knees, and I toppled over. Through blurred vision I glimpsed the pig snorting like it was going to charge again. The Arab kid cried, "No! No!" I whisked the pig's snout off with my knife and a tinkle of blood sputtered from its face, and then *clack*—Jesus shot it in the head with his Beretta.

Rachel said, "Goddammit. Leave the kid alone. This is seriously fucked up."

Jesus cried, "Oh shit," pointing behind me with his smoking pistol.

I spun and spotted a Bedouin in a brown cloak with his musket sighted on me. The first shot rang out, like a church bell, and wheat cinders exploded to our left. A *piff* of smoke came up off the Bedouin's rifle tip. There was an ominous rustle and thirty Bedouins stepped forward out of the wheat, all training rifles on us. There were more *piffs*. We beat it out of there, with the Bedouins hot on our tail.

▪ ▪ ▪

We crashed into a ditch and set up our rifles facing out. Some of the Bedouins were scattering and trying to circle around us on all fours. We'd been caught with our pants down, and now all our gear and radios were back at the shack. Without communication, exfiltration was a no-go. I flipped up my telescopic sight and saw a gang of kamikaze Bedouins streaming toward us with their rifles blazing. Thrash and Rachel and Jesus were dropping targets with lead, very methodical. Enemy fire ripped the air around my head and the ditch was choked with smoke. I polished off my last magazine. Rachel yelled, "Fuck," and spiked her M-16 in the dirt. One of the Bedouins geronimoed into our hole, and Jesus whirled and stabbed him in the neck.

"Grenades," said Thrash. We each kept a grenade in our cargo pocket so that we could step out of this world on our own terms. We glanced at one another and pinched the pins on our grenades, opening the door to eternity. There was so much smoke, and I felt my head spiral up into the air, and suddenly the screaming seemed very far away, and I thought for a second that I was already dead. I said a jumbled, silent, nondenominational prayer, trying to cover all my bases.

The scream of a train's whistle ripped my prayer to shreds. I opened my eyes and saw an old train trudging down the tracks, headed south. Without a word, we scrambled to stick the pins back in the grenades.

Thrash whispered in a frantic voice, "I threw my pin away." I glanced up and saw Thrash clutching the grenade with this helpless look on his face and my heart went out to him. Thrash leapt from the ditch and erupted in midair, spraying the charging Bedouins with blood and chunks of flesh. Thrash's right hand, violently emancipated from the rest of his body, shot out and slapped one of the charging Bedouins in the face. The Bedouin bent over and vomited. Several charging Bedouins were blown backward up off their sandaled feet. We raced along the train. Rachel and Jesus hopped into a boxcar. It was a lumber shipment: there were stacks of boards and wood in the car. The first time I leapt for the open door of the boxcar, I miscalculated and cracked my jaw and bounced off into the dirt, but then instantly scrambled up and raced and dove with everything I had into the open door.

The day after Sandra's therapist, Kevin, told Sandra to start stripping for her self-esteem, she went down to Brad's for an audition. Sandra has a body like you would not believe: big, round breasts, perfect quarter-size nipples that you could gouge an eye out on, and down below—I cannot even talk about down below. Shaved, completely. Brad hired her on the spot, and by the next week she had bought, because of her R.N. joke, a skimpy nurse's outfit and come up with this routine. She did things to herself with a stethoscope. I remember one day Thrash sidled up to me while we were practicing land navigation, and said, "Whoa. Do you know about Sandra? I saw her last night at Brad's. Man, I felt guilty being there. I had to leave." I could not tell him why she was there, that it was part of her therapy, so I lied and said we had some bad credit debt, and that it was good money.

Jesus said we had to sneak back to the village and try to recover the gear, or our asses would be in a sling. So at dusk we hopped off the train and flew up the highway. At about 0200 we elected to rack out for a couple hours before the big raid, but first we built a little fire and sat around it in a circle.

"Thrash was a good guy." Rachel seemed really upset. "I just can't forget the look on his face."

"He definitely looked surprised," I said.

"You're an idiot, Frank," said Rachel. She winked. "But you're not all bad."

A little while later my eyelids started to droop, and I heard Rachel ask Jesus what it was like to have his name. "I've always wanted to ask," she said.

Jesus said, "You want to hear something funny. I don't believe."

Rachel said what about the Bible, what about Mary and Gabriel and all that. Because she said she probably believed.

Jesus snorted, and said the Bible was just a *crucifiction,* with a *C.* "Just a story to keep the majority in check. It's a conduct code. Either that, or it's really just the all-time greatest what-to-name-your-baby book," he said, and I drifted off to the sound of his chuckling.

And I was jerked awake by his shout for help.

Rachel and I sat up in our hooch, and we instantly scrambled out to where the fire was still smoldering. Jesus, who was supposed to be standing watch, was nowhere around. There were a few drops of blood in the sand, and some drag marks that disappeared after a couple of feet. We bounded out into the night and the waves of dunes stretched forever, and there was no wind, and the sound of our boots pounding on the sand was muted, like we were on the moon. Rachel abruptly stopped and panted, "Wait. I hear something." She bent over, hands on knees.

A low moan zoomed out from behind this giant dune.

Rachel locked her eyes on mine, and said, "Stay here." Then she slid to the ground and low-crawled toward the dune, and I watched the soles of her boots disappear over the peak. "Why should I stay here," I whispered to myself, just as Rachel started screaming.

"Oh God! No! Holy Christ! Good God, no!"

I rushed up the dune but stopped short at the top of it. The Arab kid had slumped Jesus's lifeless body up against a tiny one-foot makeshift cross he had constructed with slats of wood I recognized from the train. Jesus looked like he was kicked back in a La-Z-Boy chair, and there was a silver hammer and nails in the sand. The kid looked up at Rachel and shouted, "Eye for eye! Eye for eye!" I wanted to puke with grief, and my mind flashed to Jesus's parents back in Puerto Vallarta, the picture they kept of Jesus in uniform by their hammock, their humble pueblo, the roosters out back crowing defiantly against their poverty. And it was not as if this was a crime of passion—the hammer and nails and wood: this was premeditated. Rachel screamed and rushed down and grabbed the hammer and went to work on the Arab kid with it. The last thing I heard the Arab kid shout was, "I'm doing you fava! You said you beleeved! Have mercy!"

She gave him what he wanted.

# Those Were Your Words
# Not Mine

## REWARD

I am blind, which is the reason I, Valerie Hackett, am having to offer this reward, and because I am blind I cannot see the keys as I type this, so please forgive me if there are any mistakes. Three weeks ago, on February 23, 1991, my nineteen-year-old son, Chad Hackett, a Navy SEAL, was killed in combat over in Desert Storm. The way I found out about this was two government men came to my room and notified me of Chad's death, while I lay here in bed.

The details of Chad's death are puzzling. According to the government men, Chad's SEAL team, stationed at Ras al Mishab, Saudi Arabia, was involved in some operation that tricked the Iraqis into believing thousands of American soldiers were storming the Kuwaiti beach of Mina Saud. Tragically, Chad's team was spotted by Iraqi defenders set in along the berm of the beach, and since they had already buried the explosives in the sand, the other SEALs hopped in their Zodiacs and paddled out. Chad, however, according to the two men, charged the Iraqi machine-gun nest. Now this is the strange part: Chad was carrying something called a Koch MP-5 machine gun, and yet he never fired a single shot as he ran at the Iraqi soldiers, who cut him down in midsprint. No one is really sure why Chad charged the Iraqis, but everyone agrees that it was very brave. The two government men said Chad was brave and courageous.

The two government men also handed over Chad's personal belongings, which they found on his body after it was recovered by his fellow SEALs. There was not much, his dog tags, an I.D. card, and a letter, which apparently was sealed in a Ziploc baggie, strapped inside his wet suit, so I assume this letter must be important. The strange thing is I asked my nurse to read me the letter, then my friends, and then my family, but all of them, after glancing at the letter, refused to read it to me. The only person who did actually "read" the letter to me was my sister Rhonda, but I could tell by the singsongy voice she used and the way she kept clearing her throat that she was not really reading the letter. She was making it up. Rhonda has always been a liar.

So whoever is reading this, someone who lives here with me in the Recovery Ward and who has come into my room and is right now reading this reward note posted on the wall next to my bed, I say this to you: **I am willing to pay $300 to the first person who will read this letter to me.** The letter itself is taped on the wall below the reward note, so please, do a kind deed for an old blind woman, and help put her heart at ease, and make $300 in the process.

THE LETTER FOUND IN MY SON CHAD'S WET SUIT

Dear Chad,

Hi love. I was so excited to get your letter today that when I snatched it out of the mailbox and saw who it was from I sprinted all the way back in the house and into my room and I called Jeannette, Pam, Megan, Uncle Stan and Aunt Judy, Mom and Dad at work, and Grandma and Grandpa Pollard in Seattle to tell them not to call me or to bother me for the next hour because I was going to be extremely busy reading this letter

that I just received from Ras al Mishab, Saudi Arabia, from my
dear sweet Navy SEAL, who is right now getting ready to storm
the beach off the coast of Kuwait.

Then I yanked down the blinds and bolted my door and
took off all my clothes (Remember when you called from the
Naval Amphibious Base the night before you got shipped over
to Saudi and you made me promise I would read all your letters
naked? You said it would be more fun to write them because
you'd know that I would be naked when I read them? Well, I
kept my promise.) and crawled under the sheets and cuddled
up with Mr. Snuggles (By the way, Rags bit a hole in Mr.
Snuggles and now some of his stuffing's coming out. Can you
believe it? I had to hit Rags with my belt. Bad Rags. Poor Mr.
Snuggles.) and had just finished the "Dear Montana" of your
letter when there was suddenly a loud banging at the front
door.

I was like, Who can that be.

So I leapt out of bed and wrapped a towel around me and
flew all the way through the living room and then I threw open
the door and you'll never in a million years guess who it was. It
was Kurt Donovan. Can you believe Kurt Donovan just showed
up at my door out of the blue like that? I thought this was so
completely weird because I know that Kurt started pre-law at
Berkeley this year and I remember right before you shipped
out you told me that when you got out of Desert Storm the first
thing you were going to do was go straight up to Berkeley and
kick Kurt Donovan's ass.

I distinctly remember you said you were going to tie Kurt
Donovan to a tree out in the woods with some special SEAL
rope and break all his teeth out one by one and then you were
going to cut off his feet and then stab him in the spine so his
legs were paralyzed, but first, you said, before you did all that,
you were going to "straight-up kick his ass." Do you remember?
You said this to me three months ago before you shipped off to

BASIC UNDERWATER DEMOLITION/SEAL TRAINING in Coronado and you knew that when you were done with that and you were officially a SEAL they were going to ship you over to Saudi because that's what your navy personnel detailer told you when he offered you the chance to go to BUDS.

Then after you said what you were going to do to Kurt Donovan you threw yourself on the ground and started doing one-armed push-ups and each time you came up you shouted, "You want some of this, you son of a bitch?" And then the next day at the bus station right before you were going to board the bus for the Warfare Center up in Coronado I asked you if you were nervous about starting BUDS because I know I would be and you said, "We'll see how Kurt Donovan likes scooting around Berkeley in a wheelchair. I bet the girls in Berkeley won't like Mr. Genius Pre-law Kurt Donovan so much when they see him scooting around town in a wheelchair. You want to bet? I'll betcha. This will be Kurt Donovan." Then you got down in a squat position and moved your arms back and forth just the way you figured Kurt Donovan would move his arms when he was in a wheelchair.

So like I said, this really surprised me, that Kurt was standing at my door like that, because I thought you and Kurt had issues, but when I mentioned this he said, "What are you talking about? What's in the past is in the past. To tell you the truth I'd forgotten all about it." And then Kurt said he had no idea that you were still mad at him for what he did in the fourth grade when he put that chocolate-covered doughnut on his dick in the cafeteria and told you that if you didn't eat the chocolate-covered doughnut off his dick then God would make your mom go blind and so you ate the chocolate-covered doughnut and threw up and everyone at your table laughed. Kurt Donovan said that that was a heck of a long time ago, and what's in the past is in the past, and like I said, he said, "Chad didn't know

that I was just goofing around and the reason I did the thing
with the doughnut was because I secretly wanted Chad to be
my friend and besides," he said, "I just got a letter from Chad
yesterday myself."

I said, "You got a letter from Chad yesterday? In Berkeley?
Chad as in Chad the Navy SEAL who is in Desert Storm?"

He said, "Yeah, that's why I'm here. He asked me to drive
down from Berkeley and see how you're holding up."

Then I told Kurt that was really weird because I had just got
a letter from you and I was just about to read it.

Then Kurt said, "So let's read it."

So then we both went back here to my bedroom and read
your letter because I wanted to know if there was anything you
might have left out in my letter that you put in Kurt's and I
knew Kurt could tell me if there was but when we were done
reading it he said no, that's basically what you said to him too.

Except of course the poems you sent me because I cried a
little when I started reading them and then Kurt asked if he
could read one of them out loud to me because he said they
were "really excellent poems," and I can see how being over in
Desert Storm is making you think about your life and the world
in a different way. My favorite poem was "Ocean Salty Like
Tears." I love how you start off by saying that sometimes while
paddling off the coast of Kuwait you "feel just like a pirate," but
that your only gold is me, Montana.

So I know you must be dying to find out because you
asked me about a hundred times in your letter and the answer
is—yes yes yes—I went to see your mom in the hospital last
week and yes after I left your mom I went to talk to
Dr. Wexley. Dr. Wexley said, "Oh, hi, Montana." Then he told
me if I can be perfectly honest with you Montana Mrs.
Hackett's operation was a disaster and even though he'd been
able to successfully do the cornea transplant the tests were

showing that your mom's body was rejecting the new corneas and he was afraid she wouldn't have her sight back when the bandages came off.

I said, "Maybe they're defective corneas."

Dr. Wexley sighed and said, "We got those corneas from the Eyebank for Sight Restoration. As far as corneas go, they're top of the line."

I said, "But who was the donor? Maybe they were depressed and shredded their corneas by crying all the time."

And then Dr. Wexley said, "Come on, Montana, don't be ridiculous. Now I know you're upset, but the only thing you can do is be strong for Mrs. Hackett, though I'm not going to say anything to her yet. There were some complications during the surgery and she's still pretty tuckered out."

So what Dr. Wexley told me broke my heart. Especially since I had just got done listening to your mom tell me how her heart had grown wings of hope and had been soaring and for the past couple nights since the operation she'd been having these wonderful clairvoyant dreams in which she could see perfectly. She said, "Twenty-twenty." She called these dreams her Premonitions of Joy. She said, "I guess these new corneas," and then pointed to all the bandages wrapped around her head, "will not only let me see in the present, but into the future too. Thank goodness that I have such a kind and generous son to make all this happen for me."

Your mom said imagine how beautiful a bright red and orange sunset would be after being blind for ten years, and that when the bandages came off she would never go to sleep again because she would be too busy looking at things and she wanted to make up for lost time. She had said it was the little things she couldn't wait to see, like a leaf, or a bird in flight. And her son when he came home from Desert Storm. She said, "I listen to what's happening over there every day," and then pointed to the radio.

And I do too, except I watch it on the TV, hoping to catch a glimpse of you even though I know that's crazy because the whole point of you being there is that nobody knows that you're wherever you are. You are like a rock star in the war, and when you get back I want you to show me how those night scopes work that you said you used when you were spying on the Iraqi convoy of missiles during airstrikes. Only no big explosions, okay? And you know how you said you escorted some Rangers in a Zodiac so you could insert them on the beach well I want you to do some insertions on my beach. I believe you when you say that you are like an invisible ghost of justice roaming up and down the coastline there in Saudi Arabia because nobody else could stay in the cold scary water all night with just their head sticking out so they can be the long arm of the American law.

Plus I know you had been praying, Chad. This is the other thing that broke my heart. I didn't tell your mom or Dr. Wexley this so you needn't worry, but I know you've been praying every night over there in Ras al Mishab that your mom's cornea transplant would be a success. And then I also just read your poem, "This Written Prayer" #26, where you talk about it. So when Dr. Wexley told me the operation had basically been a disaster I broke down crying near the registration desk. I really fell apart. And I don't know what happened next but I guess I started to hyperventilate and I must have reached across the desk and grabbed a pair of scissors and cut my hair off because finally a bunch of nurses had to jump on me and drag me away. When I calmed down I tried to leave the hospital but the nurse showed me a piece of paper I signed while I was hyperventilating which said legally I couldn't leave the hospital, and so I spent the night strapped down in bed.

I don't think you'll mind what I'm about to tell you but if you do please hear me out before you get upset. A couple minutes ago I had Kurt Donovan's dick in my mouth. Now please don't go getting freaked out because I had Kurt

Donovan's dick in my mouth until you have read all of this letter because by the time you're done reading this letter you'll realize that I love you with all my heart and that what I'm doing right now I'm doing for us and besides, if nothing else, I want you to know that I am being completely honest with you which when you called from the Warfare Center right before you shipped off to Saudi is what we agreed was the most important thing in the world.

Do you remember, Chad, when you said on the phone, "Montana, you are the most beautiful girl in the world, and I feel like the luckiest guy in the world, and I swear I want to spend the rest of my life with you. But this is going to be tough on us. Me going over to the Middle East is going to be tough on us. And the only way we can get through this is if we are one hundred percent honest with each other." So I am being completely honest with you right now and the reason I gave Kurt Donovan a blow job is because I wanted to feel as close as possible to you I wanted to feel like you were right here with me, I miss you so much, baby.

Now this was Kurt's idea but I have to say after he talked it through with me it seemed to make a lot sense. Kurt said he would just be acting. Kurt said he would just be playing the role of Chad Hackett so that I could feel as close as possible to you. I have to confess the whole idea of it, being that close to you, made me excited so I said, okay Kurt, let's get that dick of yours out of those pants, but first we agreed that I could only put his dick in my mouth and suck on it if I promised that the whole time I would be thinking of you. So I promised, and I want you to know that I was thinking of you only moments ago when I was pretending that Kurt Donovan's dick which was in my mouth was really your dick in my mouth. I could taste your dick and it was so good, baby. That's right, in my mind Kurt's dick doesn't even exist, and you have the biggest dick in the world.

I want you to be careful over there and take care of yourself, Chad. That story about you guys capturing that whatever-whatever place and planting the flag in it was amazing. But it also sounded scary, when you described those sea mines floating all over and under the water and that at first you thought it was a sea turtle. The creepiest part was when you were finning underwater and saw that dead Iraqi soldier stuck in the barbwire and there were chunks of his leg missing like something had been eating him. I don't know why you had to pull his mask off like that and look at his face because a dead man's face is nothing good to see.

One thing I was worried about was that the operation had rattled your mom's brain loose. I figured maybe whatever they did to her eyes accidentally got her wires crossed because your mom seemed to be under the impression that I had changed my name to Abby. She would say, "These are great brownies, Abby. How is the baby, Abby? I'm so happy for you, Abby." And of course I felt so sorry for her sitting there with those bandages wrapped around her head and now she had brain damage too that I didn't have the heart to correct her. I kept my big mouth shut. I said to myself, "Mrs. Hackett has had enough sorrow in her life. So, Montana, you do not need to be the one to tell her that she has brain damage too. You just keep your big mouth shut, Montana."

God must be listening, Chad, so I wouldn't give up hope yet, and I promised I wouldn't tell anyone about why your mom is blind and I have kept my promise and I am only bringing it up to remind you how you said if God listened once then He's going to listen twice. Those were your words not mine. You said as you stood there in the center of all that laughter you realized that you hated your mom because it was her fault that you'd eaten the doughnut. You hated your mom because of how much you loved your mom. And you told me how that night your mom yelled why did she have to be the mother at work who got a call from the principal of her son's school. She shook you and screamed, "Why? Why? Why?" And you couldn't tell her you'd thrown up because you tried to protect her and your dad wasn't there to protect her because he was dead from stepping on a bouncing betty in Da Nang, Vietnam, and so it was just the two of you all alone helpless in that crappy apartment and so you decided right then and there that you completely hated her guts.

And that night you prayed to God. I hope this doesn't hurt too much to bring up but you said that night you prayed to God for assistance because you said your soul was in great distress and you needed His assistance. You prayed the way they taught you to in church. You were just a little boy and you got down on your knees and prayed to God and asked Him to make your mom go blind.

But you were just a little boy and so you shouldn't blame yourself because there's no way you could have known the next morning your mother would wake up and tell you to call the doctor because she couldn't see and then later that day an ophthalmologist would tell her that she had congenital hereditary endothelia dystrophy because how many people have ever heard of congenital hereditary endothelia dystrophy when nobody in your family has ever had it before?

I'm glad that you were thinking of me and asked Kurt Donovan to come over to my house and check up on me because I don't want you to worry or anything while you're busy getting ready to storm the beaches of Kuwait but I'd been feeling pretty down and out to tell you the truth. I don't tell you things because I don't want to worry you. But I am definitely feeling a lot better than I have been for the past few days, in fact, I have to say that this is about the best I've felt since that little incident at the hospital.

Earlier when I said I cut all my hair off in the hospital I

guess I lied. Because the person whose hair I really cut off was Abby. You are probably just as surprised to hear this as I am. This was the first time I ever heard of this Abby person and when she showed up in the doorway of your mom's room and she said, "Hi, Mrs. Hackett," and I saw the confusion on your mom's face and when I saw how big Abby's body was with a baby in it, well I put two and two together, Chad, and I just basically flipped out and I cut all of Abby's hair off or at least as much as I could get off before the nurse pulled me away. You had been two-timing me, Chad Hackett. We've been together for close to a year and now I find out you cheated and lied to me and now you've made a baby with this bitch Abby.

Kurt was just saying tell Chad I feel like a SEAL. Oh yeah I feel like a Navy SEAL. Kurt was saying how does that feel to have a Navy SEAL in my mouth like that? Kurt was saying, oh God, Montana, that's right, baby. Then I knew Kurt was about to finish. I also knew Kurt was lying when he said he got a letter from you, Chad. I just want you to know that I am being completely honest with you right now. I knew exactly what Kurt was up to when he said he got a letter from you.

My first idea was to come over there to Ras al Mishab and shoot you myself. I cannot even tell you all the things I had planned to do to you but then the more I thought about it the more I realized how sad your life has been. I know things haven't been easy with just you and your mom scraping by like that on her disability checks and I started to feel sorry for you and then I got mad at myself for feeling sorry for you because of what you did to me and I ripped Mr. Snuggles's head off and then I hit Rags with my belt.

I figure all the pain in this world must have just made you out of your mind crazy, Chad. You must have just lost your reason, you probably didn't even know what you were doing because of how crazy you were. So I forgive you, Chad

Hackett. Because we are even now and now everything
can be fine between us and I want you to know that I have
forgiven you.

But there is one last thing I want to say to you though I hope
there's no reason for me to have to say it. Don't you dare think
about trying to hurt me through God while you are over there
in Saudi Arabia. I know you and I know after you get this letter
you might be angry and do something you regret later like say a
prayer to God asking Him to do something horrible to me like
make me go blind. I'm warning you don't bother trying to get in
touch with God because I have taken care of that and I have
already said a little prayer myself.

I asked God to guard over me. I told God how I was just a
young girl in the world and all alone and how my boyfriend
Chad Hackett broke my heart and cheated on me and I told
God that if Chad Hackett from San Francisco asks Him to do
something horrible to me then He should just do to Chad
Hackett whatever horrible thing it is that Chad Hackett asks
Him to do to me. So, Chad, if you ask God to make me go blind
then what God will do is instead of make me go blind He will
make you go blind, Chad. Right there in Saudi Arabia. It was an
I'm-Rubber-You're-Glue prayer, Chad, so please don't do
anything rash because God likes women better and I am a
woman, Chad. You will learn better than to mess with a woman,
Chad.

If you don't believe me then just take one guess why it was
that Kurt Donovan showed up on my doorstep like that when
he did? The reason is because I said a prayer to God three
nights ago asking Him to send Kurt Donovan all the way from
Berkeley over to my house today so I could make things right. I
got down on my knees and I said, "I have to make things right
between Chad and me, and God you are the only one who can
help me. So, God, will you please send Kurt Donovan over to
my house three days from now because even though I don't

want to do what I am going to do, I have to make sure
everything is right between Chad and me."

So that's another reason why you shouldn't give up hope on
your mom's new corneas and why you should just accept things
as they are, because God does listen and things could be worse
and I love you. It'll all work out just fine, you'll see, and we'll be
able to put all of this behind us, and when you get done over
there in Saudi Arabia you can come straight home to me and I
swear to you I will have figured out a way to steal that baby
from Abby by then and we'll be able to start a family. In the
meantime, I'll practice signing my name as Mrs. Hackett and I
will be thinking of you and wishing that you are safe and well
over there in Saudi Arabia. I miss you and love you so much.

                                          xoxoxo ad infinitum,
                                          Montana

# Notes from a Bunker Along Highway 8

■

I know this is going to sound corny, at least to all the angry, cynical people in the world, but they can go to hell, because in the midst of everything that has happened with this screwy-ass war, yoga, and the deep concentration that I attain through yoga, has pretty much saved my life. I am probably a little addicted to it, but Dithers says that I'm a complete fruitcake, and that yoga isn't going to save my butt from getting caught and thrown in the brig. Dithers says it's my queer dad that's the reason I like yoga so much. Just recently Dithers shouted, "G.D., you know they're going to find us. You know Captain has men on us right now. It's just a matter of time. And when they find us, I'm going to be laughing my ass off at you."

I was crouched in the Wide Galaxy pose with my eyes closed, and pretended not to hear him.

"I know you hear me, G.D."

The Wide Galaxy is my favorite pose. It's the pose I like to finish with at the end of a sequence. I raise my palms to the sky, which is really just the concrete ceiling of this bunker, allowing "my hands to become my eyes," and victoriously breathe in 1-2-3-hold, and exhale 1-2-3-4-hold, and after fifteen minutes in the Wide Galaxy, my mind is right up into the void, and I feel truly shocked with bliss, grateful for the existence of every single atom in the universe.

"Hey, G.D. Hey, Zen Master. If you're looking for love, I'm your man. Come and get me."

I opened my eyes, blinked, and strolled over to the far end of the bunker, and, with my e-tool, banged on the wood slats of Dithers's cage very hard. The chimps erupted into a chorus of screeches and started shaking the slats of their cages, which pretty much sealed the deal for me: getting my head up into the void was obviously out of the question now. So, choosing to ignore Dithers's laughter, I ambled down the hall and flung back the hatch and hoisted myself out of the bunker. I went for a walk in the cool desert night, where I mentally reprimanded myself for letting Dithers get the best of me.

But I should explain: I am not by nature a violent man, not anymore anyway. I believe in the sanctity of all people. And now my only allegiance is to Life, that golden kaleidoscope which turns always in circles, riddled as it is with its patchworked bits of magic and beauty. Here in my underground bunker, which is where I am writing this from, and which was abandoned by Iraqi soldiers well before I ever arrived on the scene, I salute Life every day to the fullest, and beyond the steel hatch of the bunker and moving fifty yards south, lies Highway 8, which is the main road that runs from Basra to Baghdad. And it is on this highway that the starving, the depraved, the war-weary Iraqi civilians, mothers carrying their dead babies, one-legged orphans, whole caravans of families with shattered faces from witnessing the catastrophic demolition of their homes and villages, the flee-ing Iraqi soldiers, not the demonic Republican Guard but the scared boys and old men forced into service by their vicious dic-tator, where hundreds of charred tanks and scorched cars line the highway and the ditches alongside the highway, still even tongues of flame reach out to lick the sky, and the noxious odor of burning human flesh chokes the air—like some kind of per-manent backyard barbecue smell—this apocalyptic highway, are making their pilgrimage on foot to the supposed safety of

Baghdad, where they'll probably be blocked from the city's gates anyway.

Now some people might call me a criminal, a traitor, or worse even, because I deserted my Green Beret brothers and my country, but they are fools, because I know now that the heart is the highest law there is. And I find that if I turn an ear inward and pay very close attention, then my heart speaks to me louder and louder each day.

So there I was, strolling along that night and chewing myself out for the Dithers thing, when I stumbled upon a kindly old Iraqi woman crawling in the ditch along the highway. This was my first patient of the night and my heart quickened. I slid my ruck off and dug out my medical kit. I got down on my knees and set this woman's mangled leg in a splint. She started to speak, but I gestured shhhh. I cleaned the infected area on her calf and picked maggots out with tweezers. I rubbed the wound down with salve, which I knew must have burned. And it was then, as I was cleaning her leg and I saw the hot tears of gratitude in her eyes, it was then that I found the peace of mind that had eluded me back in the bunker.

## HUNTING FOR SCUDS,
## AND HOW I HELPED PREVENT
## A NUCLEAR WAR

It doesn't matter who you are, at some point something will happen to you out of the blue and your life will instantly be changed dramatically and forever. There's the crackle of lightning, the clouds part, and you see a muscular arm reach down and the Big Guy in the Sky deals you The Card. Well, I got The Joker. And it's funny, because once you realize the joke's on you, the last thing you want to do is laugh. And so it was for me, though even looking back on it all now there still doesn't seem to have been any sign of what that night had in store. This is how it started:

Our team was on patrol up near Al Haqlaniya, right along the banks of the Euphrates River. I was behind the wheel of the Land Rover, and Marty was scoping the landscape with his thermal sight. Our mission was to hunt and destroy SCUDs deep inside Iraq, and let me tell you, a SCUD is almost as dangerous as a BB gun, and definitely less accurate. They have no guidance system, and so the Iraqis just point them in a general direction and presto: off goes a deadly SCUD. Of course, our gazillion-dollar Patriots, courtesy of that genius Reagan, are just as ridiculous, because when a SCUD starts to drop it shatters into a thousand little parts of scrap metal, and when we fire a Patriot it just locks in on one of those little pieces, and those jerkoffs claim they shot down a SCUD. CNN runs the story, then everyone back home waves their flag, and the whole thing starts to remind you of a professional wrestling match.

"Hey," said Marty, "what's up with this shit detail?"

"You're stopping a nuclear war," said Dithers, "so quit your bitching. You're going to be able to tell your grandchildren about this."

That was our little joke. The thing about the nuclear war. Over a month ago now, January 14, some dozen SCUDs smashed into Tel Aviv and Haifa. Next thing you know Israeli prime minister Shamir aims mobile missiles armed with nuclear warheads at Iraq. The Saudis stated in no uncertain terms that if Israel got involved in Desert Storm, then they'd yank their ally status. Bush convinced Shamir to hold off starting a nuclear war by sending his best men, Green Beret, behind Iraqi lines for the sole purpose of SCUD busting.

"Yo," said Marty, pointing. "What's that? I think those might be SCUDs."

We turned and saw a stoic shepherd surrounded by teeming sheep. The shepherd angrily waved his cane at us. He was Bedouin, and these guys hated us. They were the black magic gypsies of the desert.

Everyone started whooping back at the shepherd. "Yeah," said Dithers, "those are some deadly-looking SCUDs. We'd better call it in."

Cynicism was at an all-time high. We'd been inserted by Pave Lows three weeks ago, and other than a couple skirmishes with some weak-ass Iraqi soldiers, there'd been no real action to speak of. And no SCUDs. Every couple days an MH-60 Blackhawk would shoot out to deliver fuel supplies and drop off our mail. It was freezing up there, with these wicked sandstorms, *shamals,* I think they're called, and we'd cruise all night in our Rover, and then hide out and catch some Z's during the day.

I jerked the wheel and said, "Hold on, gents." I started cutting sharp circles around the sheep. They panicked, bleating, scrambling every which way, some tumbling on their faces and others trampling them. The next thing I know, I hear a rifle shot, and Marty says, "Damn." I look over and there's a blotch of blood on Marty's shoulder. But there was no time, another shot, and our right front tire exploded, and in a blur I wrestled with the wheel as the Rover swerved and rolled up on its side. I tumbled out and aimed my Beretta at the shepherd, who was sighting in on us with a rifle. Then, and this is like nothing I've ever seen, seven or eight of the sheep stand up on their hind legs and cast off their wool coats, and I see that underneath are Iraqi soldiers brandishing AK-47s. A volley of machine-gun fire cut the dirt around our position, *tink-tink-tink* in the Rover, and I lunged and radioed our SAS counterparts for backup.

Some of us scurried through the smoke and dove and set in on the backside of a little dune. Diaz was calling in our coordinates to air support. I heard a buzzing sound and saw a team of SAS on motorcycles coming up in the rear. I was lying on heavy fire with my Heckler, and next to me Dithers was blasting rapid-fire bursts with his SAW. A feather of smoke curled up off the tip of Dithers's SAW. "Your barrel!" I shouted. "You're melting." And that's when I saw the moonlit shadow fall in the sand in front of me, and that's when Dithers let out an earsplitting scream. I rolled over just in time to see the Iraqi soldier lunging at me, driving his WWII-style bayonet glittering with Dithers's blood right at my chest. Dithers's arm had been sliced off and was lying in the sand off by itself, and the hand of the arm was still clutching the barrel he'd been trying to change out.

There was a chain-saw buzz and an SAS dude in a black jumpsuit plowed into the Iraqi with his motorcycle, planting him in the sand next to me. The Iraqi was doing the funky chicken, flopping around like something neural had been severely damaged. I looked at Dithers and a red flower of blood had begun to bloom at his armless shoulder socket. "Oh Jesus! Oh Jesus!" he cried out. "I can't feel my legs! Oh Jesus! I'm so cold! I'm so cold!" Now there was blood everywhere. Blood on Dithers, blood in the sand.

"Hang in there, buddy! Just relax! You're okay! Just relax, Dithers!"

## MY VISION OF GEORGE WASHINGTON, AND THE ENSUING EPIPHANY

Then, and I don't know why I did this, I glanced up for a split second, and I saw George Washington right out there in the middle of all the smoke and chaos. He was shirtless, sitting in a wooden hot tub with his arms draped around two blond Bud Girls in bikinis. There was a patch of fuzzy white pubic hair on his chest. I saw a half-eaten burrito perched on the edge of the tub. George had his head tilted back in open-mouth laughter, with the moonlight winking in his giant ivory teeth, but suddenly he stopped and looked at me and his face lit up, and he said, "*There* you are. I've been looking all over for you, G.D." He smiled. "Come," he said, and lifted one hand and nonchalantly waved me over, mafioso style. "You must be tired. Come reap some of the rewards of all your toil on the battlefield, son. This is

Carrie and Belinda." The girls giggled. Washington held up an apple. "We're going to bob for apples. How does that sound? You want to bob for apples? I sure could use your help, son, because I don't think I can handle it alone, if you know what I mean?" he said with a wink, and gestured expansively, spreading his arms wide behind the girls' shoulders. Just then a young African American man strolled up behind George carrying a tray on which were three silver goblets, and said, "Yous ready fo y'alls drinks, mastah?"

Dithers screamed. I glanced down at Dithers, and when I looked back up George Washington was gone. And that's when the weight of it all—the senselessness of war, the absurdity of America and its ideals, its bloody history of oppression, its macho Christian religious certainty—finally came flooding into my mind like a great white ray of liquid light. What the hell am I doing here? I asked myself. How can you defend a country that slaughtered the entire Native American race, a civilization older and more majestic than we'll ever know? A country so fucked up that its citizens killed one another over their inalienable right to keep African Americans in bondage. And where does the word *love* fit into all this? Then I gave myself the answer: You are a goddamn fool.

So right then and there, with the unshakable resolve of a man who has had the blinders ripped from his eyes after wandering for so long in complete darkness, I scooped up Dithers, who'd passed out by then, and started to walk off. Marty, firing his pistol desperately, glanced at me and shouted, "G.D., what're you doing?" There were maybe twenty Iraqis now, firing and advancing on our position, rushing up and hitting the sand on the fly. Dead sheep littered the landscape like fallen clouds. I could hear screams, weapons cooking off, motorcycles, sheep bleating, but in a sense, it already seemed far away. I kept walking, picking up my pace, and glanced over my shoulder. Marty shouted again. "Hey, G.D., get your ass over here, motherfucker.

What're you doing?" Marty was on his feet now, still firing his pistol. I slung Dithers over my shoulder and started to jog, looking back at Marty. As Marty was glaring at me, a flying Iraqi bum-rushed him and they were instantly grappling in a sandy commotion till death did they part. And then, with Dithers slung across my shoulders in the fireman's carry, I fled for my life, south, my heart in my throat, away from the fighting and chaos, leaving Dithers's arm and Green Beret behind me forever.

## MY DAD THE VIETNAM HERO, WHO NOW READS CHOMSKY, PLUS DAD'S VIGILANT ANTIWAR PROTEST

Everybody in Green Beret knows about my dad. He's a distinguished Green Beret alum, with a Medal of Honor from Vietnam, and you can find his name on the Wall of Fame at the Special Forces Training Center in Fayetteville. Like a lot of veterans, Dad never talked about The Nam. Whenever I asked him about it he'd tell me to shut up. And when Desert Storm started and we were called up, my dad wrote a letter to my commanding officer, Captain Larthrop, telling him that as a former Green Beret he vehemently opposed America's participation in Desert Storm. He quoted Noam Chomsky's famous essay "The Invisible Flag," which apparently states among other things that the Invisible Flag "waves for all of humanity." And my dad wrote Larthrop that he couldn't sit by and watch American boys get bogged down in another Vietnam quagmire, another "intervention," and so as an act of protest—he has a twisted sense of humor—he was coming out of the closet, was turning gay. He wrote me a letter explaining the whole thing. He informed me that he'd taken a lover, a forty-six-year-old criminal lawyer named Rob whom he'd met at his yoga class at the Y. The same Y we used to do yoga together at when I was growing up. I felt betrayed. He said Rob had been openly gay for his entire life and that Rob was being a great support during the transition period. The whole letter was Rob this and Rob that, like I was supposed to be grateful or something.

I wrote my dad back. Lots of times. I begged him to reconsider his position. I used whatever logic suited my argument. I told him first and foremost that what he was doing was an affront to the gay community, and that he should be careful about what his method of protest implied. I sent him articles clipped from *Science* magazine explaining how gay people had no more choice over their sexual preference than heterosexual people did, that it was all genetics. He wrote me back to inform me that he'd just sent a letter to Jesse Helms's office, suggesting that North Carolina make a motion to legalize gay marriages. He said, Maybe I'm jumping the gun here, but this is the happiest I've been in years. I sent him a *Times* article describing the vicious underground militia of the gay organization B.P.C., Better Population Control, and that he should watch out because they'd be pissed if they heard about the mockery he was making of their sexual orientation. He sent me back a full-color photograph of a naked blue-eyed man sitting on a porous rock on a beach in Jamaica that had been clipped from a magazine called *Out*, and scrawled at the bottom of it in my dad's handwriting was: "This is still a free country, right?" And he'd drawn a little smiley face.

That last letter took the wind out of my sails, and I didn't write him back. I guess I also thought it would blow over, but my dad called the *Raleigh News and Observer* and they broke the story. The story spun, and it suddenly got a ton of media play. A highly decorated Vietnam soldier, former Special Forces with a Medal of Honor, as an act of protest, announces that he will be gay until every single American boy is home safely. My dad was a guest on all the TV and talk-radio shows, liberal, right wing, it didn't matter to him, he was just looking to get his message out. Rush Limbaugh had a field day with it, brought him and Rob on his TV show for an interview. I didn't watch it, but Dithers did. Dithers said the title of the show was "American Hero Bends Over for Peace."

My dad's got a pretty good sense of humor, so he wore a wry grin the whole time and busted jokes and kept the aggressive audience in stitches, is what Dithers said. When it comes to being a wiseass, you really can't mess with my dad.

## DITHERS'S DANGEROUS COMA, AND THE INADVERTENT DISCOVERY OF BUNKER

With Dithers slung across my back in a fireman's carry, I fled south along the foamy bank of the Euphrates. I ran for hours and hours, not stopping to think about the magnitude of what I'd just done, afraid that if I did I might lose my nerve and turn back around. The cold night wind bounced off the water and blew through my bones, and in the chaos of my mind I hoped maybe it would sweep me up like a kite and carry me to a land far, far away from there. Dithers had slipped into a dangerous coma, and I kept stopping to douse his wound with water, and then patched it up as best I could with a T-shirt. Then it was more shuffling, guided by the North Star. I can't remember much from that time. I recall a rock I camped under at the bank of the river, and I remember Dithers coming to at one point and shouting, "Help," and then passing back out. It was well into the second night that I saw from a distance the great paved highway with the fires blazing alongside it. I was gasping for air as I came up to the edge of the highway. I heard someone shout in Arabic, and the flash of a muzzle lit up next to the skeleton of a bombed-out car. "Stop," I shouted. *"Salaam alaikum!"* Which is the only Arabic I know, and it means "peace be with you." A whole slew of flashes erupted, and the sand around my feet was jumping in the air, making it difficult to see. I didn't have any fight left in me, and I resigned myself to whatever happened, and in a way, that desperation is what gave me courage, I knew nothing could hurt me now as I scrambled to the other side of the six-lane highway in a flurry of enemy fire, nothing, that is, except for an errant round that shaved off a quarter inch of my kneecap. The pain exploded up my spine, and my brain went wet with shock and fear. Even now I've got a slight limp. I collapsed facefirst into the sand, using Dithers to break my fall. I got to one knee and dragged Dithers behind the cover of two huge boulders, and that's when I spotted the steel in the sand. One of the Iraqi was blowing a whistle very loudly, and there were shouts, and I heard the men moving in my direction. I pulled back the steel hatch, and threw Dithers in first, and then I jumped down in, pulling the hatch to. The fall was about ten feet, and Dithers and I landed in a heap on the ground. It would only be later that I found the steel ladder fastened to the wall. I heard the soldiers shouting in Arabic up above. I held my breath in fear, and my heart knocked on the door of my rib cage. I saw the milk white of my kneecap where the bullet had shaved off the skin and felt woozy. Finally the soldiers up above us moved on. It was only then that I noticed the horrible stench of the place. Screeching sounds erupted from what sounded like the center of the earth. With Dithers in my arms like a newlywed, I ventured cautiously down the hall, casting the beam of my flashlight over the concrete walls.

## THE CHIMPANZEES WHO WERE HERE BEFORE US

Something furry crashed on my head as I crossed the threshold, and a cacophony of screeches erupted, reverberating off the inside of my skull, threatening to split it down the middle. I envisioned the dust that my brain had become spilling out. Dithers fumbled out of my arms, and I felt leather hands pounding and tugging at me. In the commotion I managed to light a flare from my cargo pocket and then I sprang to my feet and shrugged off my attackers, and in the fiery shadows I saw several chimpanzees screeching at me and waving their fists over their heads. Their yellow eyes were filled with hate. Like everyone else I'd seen the psyops pamphlets Iraq had dropped with a picture of King Kong eating the heads of terrified American soldiers, but I never thought there was anything to it. I spotted Dithers motionless on the floor in a heap. His forehead was pale and slick with sweat. His shoulder was a gory red flesh mess, and I realized he could be dead. I shouted, "Getouttahere!" and waved the flare around in my hand like a sparkler and then frantically chased the chimpanzees into the back of the bunker with it.

The bunker looked as if it had been abandoned in a hurry. Later, once I'd found the light switch, I also discovered the pinewood cages and figured out that the chimps must have escaped after the Iraqis deserted the bunker. There was a giant metal table against the south wall, which was strewn with papers and booklets that I can't read, but, judging by the pictures and illustrations, are booklets that describe how to make chemical weapons. And there's the hand-to-hand combat stuff, and an English dictionary from 1964. In the closet I found a big box of M.R.E.s. There was also a giant cache of weapons, but there's no ammo. RPGs, AK-47s, M-16s, the works. On the north wall is a little bathroom area complete with toilet and sink. And a couple lightbulbs dangle from the ceiling. And like I said, the wooden cages, eight total, stacked up on one another, pushed up against the east wall.


## HOW I CAME TO BE KNOWN AS G.D.

This was at Fort Bragg, North Carolina. We were rehearsing hostage rescue. My team crashed through the third-story window, and I hit the deck, laying on cover fire with my 9mm, while Dithers scurried forward with Marty to search the bedrooms and bathroom and laundry room. A robot, The Dad, came rushing in from the kitchen, crying out, "Help, help, they've got my son." A three-dimensional hologram of a German shepherd appeared on the wall. The dog started barking at me and baring its teeth, threatening to compromise our mission, so I blew its head off with my 9mm, and synthetic blood splattered everywhere. The graphics were amazing. I leapt up and moved swiftly to The Dad, reciting my lines, "We're here to help, sir. Please lie down on the floor under a table until further instructed. You are safe now." I was in midspeech, on the word *table*, when Dithers dove back into the room, squeaking, "Hit the deck, hit the deck!" as he sprayed The Dad with his Koch MP-5 series machine gun, so that the robot's chest ripped open and a fuse shorted and blazed momentarily, and then the machine's lights went out. I turned to Dithers, and blurted, "What the hell?" But he was already beside The Dad, and he yanked off The Dad's face, revealing the grinning, pockmarked mannequin face of the Middle Eastern Terrorist (MET) we'd been instructed to terminate. A baby in diapers waddled out from the kitchen, and I said, "Here's number one. Got 'im," and scooped him up, then sprinted into the kitchen, where the baby's dad was lying, apparently bludgeoned by the MET with a toaster. The father gasped, "You took too long, and now I will die because of you. If I were a real person you would now have to live with the burden of my death for the rest of your life, soldier." Marty came bursting through the kitchen door and I jumped and the baby dropped from my arms, landing on its head. "You moron," shouted Marty. The baby started howling like a fire engine, and Captain Larthrop's crackly voice came on over the intercom. "Christ Almighty, son, where the fuck is your head? Good job, Dithers, but it looks like the real terrorist here is you-know-who." You-know-who was me. "Grab your gear and get in the frigging debriefing room, you knuckleheads."

On the way to the debriefing room, Marty turned to me and spat, "Nice job, Mr. Gay Dad. Next time why don't you just hug the MET to death." Dithers started laughing, and said, "Yeah, *G.D.* Why don't you give him a big kiss next time," and it was with that laughter that my new name was born.

## DITHERS'S NEAR-DEATH EXPERIENCE, AND MY SPIRITUAL CONVERSION TO THE ART OF HEALING, NOT HURTING

It was touch and go for a week or so there, but then I finally got Dithers to regain consciousness. Snatched him right out of the jaws of death is how I like to think of it. Those first couple days I tended to him around the clock. He was shaking and his teeth were chattering and not once did he open his eyes. I gingerly pulled back his eyelids with my thumbs and saw nothing but white. I thought maybe hypothermia and shock. I squeezed perfect droplets of water into his mouth with a wet rag. Endlessly wiped his damp forehead with leaves. Changed his soiled skivvies. He'd lost a ton of blood. I patched up his shoulder with gauze dressing from my medical kit. When the gauze was saturated red I would change it out. I changed and I changed and I changed. On the third day the bleeding stopped. Just like that. And throughout all this I would talk to Dithers in his fevered state, words of consolation.

"Hang in there, Dithers," I'd whisper into his ear. "You're in for a little shock, buddy. You've lost your right arm. But you shouldn't worry about it, even though some people are going to think you're a one-armed freak, screw them. Do you know why, my friend? Because that missing arm is a symbol. It's a symbol of the sickness you left behind when you quit the war." Then I would pause to let all this sink in, before going on. "You don't know yet that you have quit the war. But Dithers, let me tell you something. You can rest easy now, buddy. Because all that stuff is behind us now. We've got our whole lives ahead of us."

When Dithers finally came to, his eyes fluttered, and then

they opened very wide as if for good. He smiled. "Hey," he said. "It's good to see you." He reached for my hand and squeezed it. "God, it's good to see you, G.D." Then he asked me where the rest of the team was. "Where is everybody?" he said, looking around. "Where are we? Hey," he said, "you're not going to try and make a move on me now, are you, G.D.? G.D.? Hey, what's wrong?" he said with a cocksure grin.

## MY DAD'S PROPAGANDA CAMPAIGN, IN THE FORM OF LETTERS SENT TO ME SINCE I'VE BEEN IN THE MIDDLE EAST

Dear Son,

You amuse me. When you say I have dishonored my country, and the uniform I served in, and the proud tradition of American Warfare, just because I prefer to make love to men rather than women, you drive home my point even further, that the biggest mistake I ever made was putting my dick inside your mother. That was truly a "dishonorable discharge." You are emblematic of everything that is wrong with your pansy, self-conscious, haven't-worked-for-anything-and-have-no-sense-of-history generation. Let me tell you something about honor. I fought the mighty Vietcong, and here you are in the Persian Gulf war, sitting in the desert, making sand castles. I piss on your war, and it has no more bearing on history than an ant's testicle. I can't wait to see the great stories your generation writes about their war. Oh boy. That's going to be fascinating. What do you know of honor, of sacrifice, of death anyway? And what are you fighting for? Oil. How dignified, how noble, how principled. What is the battle cry over there, "Fill 'er up?"

So I could care less if your team is making fun of you for having a gay dad. I broke dink necks with my bare hands because I could, danced with a dead gook in my arms for an entire night while smashed out on opium. I saw a boy from Georgia keep himself alive by holding his guts in his hands. You tell Marty or Dithers or anyone else from your team that if they were here with me right now, I would bend them over and "break them off something."

Now listen, son, let me give you a piece of advice. It sounds like you are all wound up over there, and that you are focused on all the wrong things. What I recommend is the next time you find yourself in a foxhole with Dithers, you get him to give you a blow job. I cannot recommend this highly enough, and I think you will instantly recognize the sagacity of my advice. Who else would know best how to give a blow job but a man? That is my one real regret. When I think back to The Nam, and consider how many lonely nights I spent, I feel the bitter taste in my mouth of lost opportunity. Of dark regret.

As ever,

Dad


## ESTABLISHING ALLIANCES, THE FIRST STEP TOWARD THE PROJECTED COALITION

It hasn't been easy getting used to these chimpanzees. What kind of disgusting creature has a carpet of pubic hair all over its body? A chimpanzee. They are dirty and they stink. I can smell them right now, which is why I tend to stay on this side of the bunker. But they're my friends, or at least they will be soon. I'm training them to be my friends.

After setting up shop here, I went ahead and named the chimpanzees, respectively: Ingrid, Ronald, Beverly, Lorraine, and Dennis. Ingrid is gentle, and the first thing she tried to do after that first bit of unpleasantness was pet my cheek. Her favorite song is "Happy Birthday." When you sing "Happy Birthday" she tries to bounce up and down on her head. Ronald likes to make kissing noises and then look around as if he didn't know where they were coming from. Beverly is deaf. It took me a while to figure out she was deaf until finally I snuck up behind her and clapped my hands. Lorraine. Well, Lorraine is the brooding-poet type—she just sits around and stares with a superior look on her face. And Dennis is a gigantic male with big biceps. I've seen Dennis amble up and mount each of the other chimps at will, girls and boys. I keep a close eye on Dennis. So you might wonder how I could be sure which are the girl chimps and which are the boy chimps. Well, this would tell me that you've never seen a chimpanzee in person before, because a chimp's penis is something that can't be ignored.

It wasn't until later that I put them back in their cages. Of course there wasn't any way for me to know if I was putting them back in their original cages, but I didn't care. A cage is a cage is a cage. At first they didn't take to the idea, and Dennis and Lorraine tried to gallop down the hall to the bunker hatch, but I've always had a quick first step and even with this bum knee I was able to get the jump on them. In fact, and I don't want to step on anyone's toes here and presume to speak on behalf of the chimps, but I'd be willing to bet that if these chimps could speak English they'd say they prefer this arrangement to the one that they had before. If for no other reason at least they're safe from Dennis now.

## I MAKE MY CASE TO DITHERS, WHO HAS SOME TROUBLE SEEING THE LIGHT, BUT EVENTUALLY COMES AROUND

The penalty for desertion is the brig. Pure and simple. The brig's where they can, because it's Military Law, strip you naked and throw you in solitary "think tanks" all in the name of Justice. If you make too much noise they'll break your jaw and then wire it shut. Standard cuisine is bread and water. I met a blind Marine once at the V.A. hospital, a young private who'd spent three months in the brig; he had a white bandage over the top of his head, and apparently a guard had conked him in the nose with a club and those things that hold your eyeballs in place had come detached. "They float every which way now," he said. "Every which way but loose," and then started cracking up. "Because check it out. They're sending me home with a medical discharge as long as I don't make a stink about it. Full benefits."

And so, because my heart tells me that I don't deserve to spend the rest of my life in the brig, I have now, metaphorically speaking, changed my identity, and so I've renamed myself Help People. Help People's my name because help people is what I do. Every night. Right after a long yoga session, after getting my mind up into the void, running through the routine of Peaceful Rainbow, Fierce Cricket, Sun Salutation, and then finishing off with Wide Galaxy, I slip out into the night with my medical kit and tend to the wounded Iraqi pilgrims littered along the sides of the highway.

And I'm a quick study. And I've learned the Ways of the Desert, so fueled on by the victorious breathing that I feel all the way down to the soles of my feet, when I go out on my nightly forays for the Good of Mankind I'm basically an untouchable phantom. The secret is to move with the land, not against it. One night I might filter myself out among the stars, and on another I might blend into the billions of grains of sand that line the desert floor. I become and do whatever's needed because I let my heart steer me through the madness now. I always wear my NVGs, night-vision goggles. I've still got all my gear: rifle, rucksack, e-tool, flak jacket, Gore-Tex, helmet, gas mask, poncho, poncho liner, maps, and of course the most important item of all, my medical kit.

So, when Dithers came out of his coma, lying there holding my hand, and started hammering me with all those questions: I told him the truth. "G.D. is dead," I said. "My name's Help People now, Dithers."

One of his eyebrows arched.

"Help People?" he said with a half grin, his voice raised.

I tried to figure out what else he needed to know. Then I spoke. "Yes. Help People. And I move with the Ways of the Desert."

His smile grew wider. "Come on, man. What are you up to? We've got to get back and blast those SCUDs, right? What about the nuclear war?" he said, grinning.

I told him about seeing George Washington. I told him how America had no real culture of its own and how that burrito was a symbol for what we'd done to our downtrodden neighbor, Mexico, how America raped other countries of their cultural artifacts and then filtered them through its sadistic and glamorous lens of ultra-consumerism. "We put everything in neon letters," I said. I told him how America was the home of the gun-toting white supremacists, and that Charlton Heston was really the Grand Wizard of the KKK. I told him that the Native Americans were living works of art and we'd murdered them. That even the term Native American was an oxymoron. I said, how can we fight for a country where only forty years ago it was no big deal to lynch an African American. My mouth ran on and on. I redressed his shoulder with gauze bandages as I talked, and I watched as the smile slid right off Dithers's face. I could see the wheels churning in his head as I talked. Finally, breathless, I stopped. And the second I stopped talking he spoke right up. What he said popped right out of his mouth as if it had been on the tip of his tongue the entire time.

"So when do we leave here, G.D., and get back to the guys?"

"We're not leaving," I said. "That's the whole point. Haven't you been listening to a word I've said?"

"I could be ready in a couple days," he said, and tentatively stretched one of his legs out. "Of course it's gonna be difficult with this," he said, and nodded to his bandaged shoulder. "But I'm willing to give it a shot." And as he said this his head slowly turned and his eyes met mine and held them.

I think the look on my face said it all. My eyes were stone that burned fire in the middle. I waited for the idiocy of what he'd just said to sink into his head. Finally he turned away and stared at the table with all the papers and books spread over it. I watched his brow furrow. His brain appeared to be chewing something over.

Then his face broke into a smile and he turned to me and said, "Well, it seems like you've been doing a lot of thinking. And I'm glad you're doing what you're doing. Help People, huh? I like that." He glanced at his armless shoulder. "Because let's face it. If it weren't for you, I probably wouldn't be alive right now." Then he looked back up at me, the smile widening. "So how about that, Help People? Say. You got any chow around here? What do we eat anyway? I'm starving."

### PROPAGANDA LETTER #2

Dear Son,

Everyone's saying Desert Storm looks like a video game on the TV, but from where I'm sitting you couldn't get me to pay a quarter to play it. Hell, I'd rather play Pong—remember how I used to kick your butt at Pong?—or pinball. I have one question for you. Is that war as boring to fight as it is to watch on TV? I sure hope not, for your sake. Because too bad for you, you can't just click the remote and flip to another channel. Rob said he wondered if the ratings sink low enough on Desert Storm, they'll yank your prime-time spot and put it on late night with all the infomercials. Have you even got to fire your weapon yet? I heard on NPR where American soldiers in Saudi

Arabia had to conserve ammunition over there, so when they practiced drills they had to make sounds that approximated the sounds of rounds being fired. I heard one grunt going, "Bata-tat-tat-tat." What kind of war is that, where you have to pretend to fire your weapon? Shit. There's more killing in the American inner cities every day then there is in your entire Desert Storm so far. Compton, California, is more dangerous than Kuwait! Maybe if you want to prove your manhood by shooting people, Mr. Bigshot, you should start dealing crack over there, then you might see some action.

Get your head out of your ass and come home, son. Have you ever thought about why you're over there in the first place? Did you know that the American government used to consider Saddam an ally in the fight against the Russians and Iran, and that we funded him and gave him weapons? That we supported him when he pulled a Hitler and gassed the Kurdish town of Halabja in 1988? America beds down with any Middle Eastern country that will do its dirty work for it. American foreign policy amounts to being a slut. Can't you see how the government is playing you for a fool? They're setting you up, son, you've inherited that myth. So don't believe it for a second.

But listen, if you do insist on fighting over there, let me give you another lesson in history. Did you know that almost all the men in Rome were gay, and did you know that the Romans were some of the mightiest warriors who ever walked the face of the earth? The reason for this is the young gay couples in love would be sent out together into the battlefield. This way, when a man took up arms, he wasn't just merely fighting for his empire, or even for his own survival; he was fighting to protect his gay lover, who was right next to him in battle—now that's what I call esprit de corps. And this ingenious mixture of love on the battlefield elicited a fierceness and aggression in the Roman soldier that could not be matched by his enemies. So, if you're still not sure, consider this: Wouldn't you be more inclined to fight to the death if Dithers were by your side, he being the man to whom you had made passionate love the night before? Just wanted to plant that thought in your head.

As ever,

Dad

## DITHERS'S GRATITUDE, AND HIS SENSE OF WONDER AND NAÏVETÉ, WHICH SEEMED TO MASK ULTERIOR MOTIVES

At first Dithers was grateful as hell to me for saving his life, and I have to admit it felt nice to be appreciated like that. Of course hiding out in this bunker took some getting used to, for both of us. But we stuck it out together, making do with what we had. It was difficult for both of us, scary even, but we toughed it out together. It's a pretty gruesome scene up there on the highway. There's packs of roving dingoes that feed off the dead. Sometimes a car will pass through, weaving around the demolished cars spilled in the lanes, rubbernecking to stop and stare at the accident. And buzzards wheeling in the sky. And that stench is sometimes too much. I have no idea what battle took place up there, but it was definitely huge. Yesterday I stumbled across a busload of civilians, lying on its side, just fully charred, and when I opened the door, I couldn't help it: I puked. I hadn't said anything to Dithers yet, but I was hoping eventually, when he was well enough, that we could start going out on these missions together. Of course that was a ways off.

And we had some good talks during that first week or so, Dithers and I. I told him more about my recent revelation, and he seemed to listen to me with much interest. I really couldn't have asked for a more attentive audience. Sometimes I'd talk to him as I cleaned the chimps' cages, making sure he watched closely, so that when the time came he'd know how to do it. He'd say, "Roger that, Help People," and, "I couldn't have said it any better myself," as he munched on a chicken à la king M.R.E. Dithers sure had worked up a huge appetite during his time in never-never land. I didn't care, though; we had more than enough chow.

But at some point I sensed Dithers wanting to get back to the killing, to the mayhem. I also got the feeling he wanted to go back and see if he could find his other arm. This was just a hunch on my part, and there was no concrete evidence that that's what was on his mind. "You know they can sew these things back on," he'd say, holding his left arm out in front of him. "I'm not complaining or anything. So don't take this the wrong way. But it sure would've been nice if you'd grabbed my arm when you split like that. Who knows? Maybe we could have sewed that thing back on." And then after some really loud bang, one of those explosions that comes every few days when the bunker rattles and little pieces of plaster flake from the ceiling and twirl to the ground, Dithers would raise up off the sleeping mat I'd set up for him and say, "*What the heck* do you think's going on out there? Huh? What do you think that was, Help People?"

His curiosity seemed to have an ulterior motive. In the mornings when I came back I'd climb down the ladder, flushed from the night's rescues, and almost land on Dithers. He'd be standing right at the base of the steel ladder, staring, I guess, up at the hatch. I knew he couldn't get out. Because whenever I left, I shoved a big boulder on top of the hatch so it couldn't swing open. I also did this to ensure that nobody on the outside would discover the hatch if they happened to be wandering around. It was a perfect, simple system. Then one morning I came back and found that Dithers had rooted through my stuff and found the maps. "Look what I found," he said. I didn't say anything. I figured he was just bored and that he'd lose interest. But then he started spending all his time looking at the maps. Too much time, as far as I was concerned. I'd come in and he'd have the maps spread out on the table, and he'd be making notations on them with his one arm. He'd look up from a map and say, "Now where exactly are we, Help People? What are the coordinates, Help People?" I hoped I wasn't being paranoid.

Eventually I had to take the maps away from him. "We are here to celebrate Life," I said, folding up the maps and putting them in my cargo pocket. Then I made a tube with my fingers and held it up to my right eye to indicate the Kaleidoscope of Life. "Who cares where we are."

His eyes glazed over, and he said, "Life, right. Sure. Definitely Life, Help People. Life." But I could tell I was losing Dithers. And I knew I was going to have to do something to help Dithers see things my way. I had to make him love his newfound life here, as I did. I knew we needed to get closer, to become friends, that this was going to take some personal investment on my part. You can't just expect someone to care about what matters to you, if they don't see that you care about them too.

## PROPAGANDA LETTER #3

Dear Son,

I mean what business does America have in Kuwait? If it's really defending certain ideals, then why don't they go to all the other places in the world where there's oppression? I'll tell you why. Because they don't have oil. The U.S. government is no better and no worse than any other government. The only difference is we've currently got the most original and innovative story in the world to guide our ship by—the Constitution. Throughout history the most successful populations have always been the best storytellers, because they know how to redress reality with a great story that justifies their cruel instincts and desire to survive. Our forefathers, those liars, those storytellers, have given America a way to feel morally justified when we do the same thing as every other country: murder, conquer, breed our population, and generate income and luxury. America the so-called big kingpin for freedom came to this land and murdered the Native Americans who were here before us. America the so-called big kingpin for freedom bought Africans from the Dutch and then kept them in chains. Don't even get me started, the contradictions are too numerous for me to note. But we're not alone in our hypocritical ways, every government is just as guilty, and so it seems like man is doomed the instant he starts to live in organized groups, but in this late stage of history, with overpopulation, man is doomed if he doesn't. That's why I've got Rob. At night, the soft moon outside the window, and with Rob's hard dick in my hand, all the worries of the world just seem to melt away.

As ever,
Dad

## MY CAMPAIGN TO RESTORE HONOR
## AND HETEROSEXUALITY TO MY DAD

I was subjected to all kinds of humiliation because of my dad. The guys would be like, "Hey, G.D., were you scared when your dad tucked you into bed at night? If he read you a story at night, what was that, like foreplay?" I was deeply ashamed, so much so that I didn't even point out that they were buying into the stupid myths that surrounded gay people: that they were more inclined to be promiscuous, that they were somehow a greater sexual threat to children. It was idiotic, but then so was my dad. Gay people were fine, in theory, but not so fine in reality, if they were your dad, who was your absolute hero. My dad had dishonored not only his service to our country but mine too. He'd made us a laughingstock. You always assume your dad won't do something to make you the butt of every joke you hear. And I didn't have the will to fight back when the guys ganged up on me, because in a sense, I knew they were right. I wanted to kill my dad for this.

Of course I'd known for a while that after Vietnam my dad had flirted with communism. I'd seen the red flags up in the attic. I knew my dad went through the disillusionment that many Vietnam soldiers did. Plus my dad had been through some hard stuff. Enter my mom. He'd met my mom in China Beach and he'd fallen in love with her, and brought her back to the States. But things went awry after that, my mom embraced Americana 100 percent and starting spending her days in the mall and at beauty salons, much to my dad's distress. They drifted apart and when I look at the pictures of her in Vietnam standing next to a moped in a miniskirt with no makeup I can't believe it's the same person. And then when my mom came home from the salon with three-inch tape-on zebra-striped fingernails, my dad went through the roof, and started shouting that's why he fell in love with her because she wasn't like the women over here, but she didn't understand. Mom didn't speak English. Finally she took it one step too far and tried to get breast implants on the sly from a doctor she'd seen on a late-night paid advertisement on TV, but there was a complication (the doctor claimed afterward that he'd warned her that 36Ds were too much for her little body frame, and then showed us the release forms she'd signed absolving him of any responsibility—the signature was the familiar X), and her heart stopped forever under the weight of all that silicone. I was sad but because of the language thing we weren't superclose. And plus I was only eight when all this happened. I do remember some things though, like how at night she'd hum pretty Vietnamese songs to me in bed and stroke my hair. So yes, my dad had definitely gone through some hard times, but that didn't do squat for my shame.

A couple days before we shipped out for Saudi, I hopped on

my motorcycle, a Kawasaki Ninja, and shot up to Raleigh, North Carolina, to put an end to all this. On the way, my hopeful thoughts muffled inside my helmet, I envisioned myself sitting down at the table and hashing everything out reasonably. I thought maybe if I let my dad know how important he was to me that would help. Maybe the whole gay thing was from low self-esteem, I thought. So I roared into the driveway and barged through the back door and spotted a man with a brown mustache seated at the dining room table, and my dad swept into the room wearing an apron and his customary rope sandals and said, "Son, what a nice surprise. I had no idea. Hey," and he opened his palms toward the mustache man, "ta-da! Here's Rob. You two have heard a lot about each other. Wow. This is a special moment." This was even worse than I thought, my dad was the femme of the relationship.

I've never liked men who wear mustaches. All my life this is something I've felt deeply. It's a gut instinct and you've got to trust those. My fourth-grade gym teacher, Mr. Jenkins, who used to come in the locker room and watch us boys change, had a mustache. My dad's brother, Uncle Ray, who was always borrowing money for his get-rich-quick schemes, had a mustache. Hitler had a mustache. In my experience a man with a mustache is someone who doesn't play fair. And this Rob character was no exception.

Rob stood up and put his arm around my father's waist, drawing him in close, and said, "Nice to meet you. We were just about to have some pancakes. Would you care for some? They're blueberry."

"In your dreams!" I shouted. "Pancakes?! Are you fucking crazy?!" I knew my face was bright red.

"Listen, you," I shouted, and I took a menacing step toward Rob. Then I told Rob in no uncertain terms that I'd be back tomorrow and that if I found him in my house I'd kick his ass from here to kingdom come. I told him that he was sick, ruining my family like this and that I'd cut off his head and stick it up his ass.

Rob sneered, "Which one is it? Are you going to kick my ass? Or are you going to stick my head up my ass? Because I don't know how my head would fit up my ass if you are busy kicking it."

My dad laughed. "Ha!" I noticed a red barn stitched on the apron he was wearing. There was a girl skipping rope in front of the barn. A friendly cow smiled from behind a wood fence. Then my dad put his hand over Rob's hand, and said, "Take it easy, Robby. I told you he'd be like that. Don't pay attention to him. He's a good boy with a good heart, just a little misdirected." I knew why my dad was laughing, and he knew I knew why he was laughing. My dad was all fun and games until he got mad, and then he was the scariest thing I'd ever seen, and there's no question that he could kick the living crap out of me if he wanted to. I couldn't believe it. My dad was taking sides. So I did the most hurtful thing I could do: I announced to my dad that from this day on, I had no dad. I said, "You're dead to me, Mr. Fag-man. I sure hope he's worth it. Because from now on you don't have a son." I instantly saw the hurt in his blue eyes, and even though part of me wanted to run to him and say, "I'm sorry," my principles wouldn't allow it. I stood my ground. He'd always been my hero, and now what he was doing was sick.

That was 107 days ago, and we haven't talked since.

## THE CAGES, AND WHY THEY ARE NECESSARY TO ENSURE PERSONAL SAFETY AND TO MAINTAIN ORDER

How I got the idea for using the cages was from Dithers. It wasn't Dithers's idea, it was my idea, but it came about because of Dithers. Because when I had to leave him to go out on my nightly missions, I realized he was still too weak to fend off the chimps. After one of my first missions for the Good of Mankind I came back and the chimps had dragged Dithers to the rear of the bunker. They were punching Dithers and jumping up and down on him. Dithers was screaming, "Help People! Help People! Help People!" When I came bounding back there, the first thing I saw was that Ingrid had Dithers's big toe in her mouth. So I put Dithers in one of the cages in the back of the main room. And it worked. I'd return in the mornings and the chimps would be screeching and banging on Dithers's cage with the empty ammo cans that were strewn around on the ground, but they couldn't get in. Then when I appeared at the base of the ladder, the chimps would scatter to the very back of the bunker. Especially since I always came in with a handful of rocks. No chimp likes to be pelted with a rock.

Eventually I just stopped letting Dithers out of the cage. It seemed like I was always coming and going, and it became too much of a hassle to be putting him in there and taking him out again and putting him in there and taking him out again. At first Dithers didn't even seem to mind, he even claimed to see the logic in it, but when his stump was almost fully healed, he started begging me to let him out of the cage.

"Look, Help People, I want to stretch my legs. I can keep things clean around here, straighten up. I'll clean the cages. I'm strong again. I can hold down the fort while you are out running your missions for the Good of Mankind. It'll make things easier on you."

"Dithers. To be perfectly honest with you, I've just grown accustomed to you being in there. I mean what if I came back and accidentally mistook you for a chimp and pelted you in the head with a rock?"

"That won't happen. How could that happen? The chimps are in their cages now. So why would you be throwing rocks?"

"Good point," I said.

Finally I relented. I didn't know for sure if I trusted Dithers. He was still acting funny, but my heart told me I had to be big and give him the benefit of the doubt. I truly believe that if you want to make progress, you have to learn to trust people. To take risks and put your faith in them. Plus Dithers did make a lot of sense. He was a lot more useful to me free than he was stuck in that cage. I was sick to death of cleaning those foul cages, and I was rewarded for my trust. Because even though Dithers had only his one arm, it turned out that he was a really good worker. It was like he used his missing arm to his advantage, as an inspiration. He got to where he could do one-armed push-ups. It was pretty damn impressive. It was as if he would do something just because he knew technically he wasn't supposed to be able to, with his disability. I respected this quality in him. Dithers even fashioned this little broom out of a board and a stick. He hummed while he swept. One time I heard him humming "Amazing Grace," which is my favorite song now, because of the lyrics. "I once was lost but now I'm found." So I started humming along with Dithers. And he looked up at me and we grinned together.

I could feel what I considered to be a real bond beginning to form between the two of us.

## A BRIEF SUMMARY OF MY MISSIONS FOR THE GOOD OF MANKIND SO FAR

I don't mean to pat myself on the back here, but this is what it's all about. Straight up. This is the justification for my very existence. And so I think it's important to keep track of all that I've done for other people. All total, I have administered medical aide to twenty-seven Iraqis, and most of them have been civilians. I put little notches into the wall of the bunker for each person I've helped.

It can be heartbreaking work, and you never know what

you're going to find. A little over a week ago I came up over a dune and found a young Iraqi man gasping for air by the side of the highway. He had a nasty sucking chest wound. He had a bushy head of hair and a big nose and a mustache. He had sensitive eyes, and they were bulging, as his head rocked back and forth. When I knelt down over him, I saw all the pores in his face.

His chest rattled each time he gasped for air and it sounded like somebody shaking a tin can with a rock in it. The lung had already collapsed, so there wasn't much I could do. It was pretty clear he was about to make the journey to the Great Beyond. Through the gaping hole in his chest, you could see his insides. His liver was a shiny white in the moonlight. It didn't seem like he even knew I was there. But I never give up hope, so I pushed down on him, getting him to exhale, and then stretched a piece of plastic over the chest. Then I slicked on the first-aid dressing over the plastic. His breathing smoothed out a little, but he also closed his eyes, which wasn't a good sign. Then I held his hand for a moment and whispered, "Go ahead, friend. There's another world out there somewhere. A world where there's no pain. A world where you can be young forever. Hurry, my brother." I shed a quick tear, which twinkled on my cheek in the moonlight, and then let go of his hand and took his rifle and went further on into the darkness.

## DITHERS'S REHABILITATION

I knew I had to go out of my way to make sure Dithers enjoyed his life here. And I knew I'd made real progress over the past couple weeks. It got to where we were talking all the time. He'd tell me about his dreams, and I'd tell him what I'd done the night before on my mission. He still wasn't, in my opinion, well enough to leave the bunker, and so of course he was really curious about what it was like up there. I'd tell him about the carnage. The innocent civilians. And he'd say, "That is seriously screwed up. I wonder if those people have any idea how lucky they are that you're around to tend to them." It was a question I'd asked myself plenty of times. I knew we were making real progress if Dithers could see things like that. I thought the day was fast approaching when we could go out together. I looked forward to it, because sometimes those nights got really lonely. And the fires by the highway burned constantly, and the sight of it all could definitely get a person down.

So I did what I could to speed up Dithers's recovery. And once while Dithers was sweeping up, I said, "Hey Dithers, have you ever tried yoga?" The chimps were fast asleep, and the peaceful atmosphere made me feel generous. Having personally benefited from the extreme results of regular yoga, I was anxious for him to reap the rewards too.

Dithers rolled his eyes. "You mean that stuff that you're always doing. The bending down and the breathing. Tying yourself up in knots stuff."

I chuckled. I hadn't thought to consider what my yoga looked like on the outside. Since for me it was such a spiritual thing. The whole point was to burrow so deep down into my body that I'd forget I even had a body. I know a lot of people say it's about self-realization, connecting the mind, body, and soul, but that's not my take on it. "Yeah," I said, grinning. "The knot stuff."

Then Dithers nodded his head and stated unequivocally that he hadn't ever done yoga, and that yoga was for fags. I opted to ignore the dig, because I knew he didn't mean it like that, that he wasn't thinking of my dad when he said it, and I asked him if he'd like me to show him some moves.

"Thanks but no thanks. Maybe in my next lifetime, Help People," said Dithers. "You just do your thing. I'll keep cleaning," and he moved into the corner, away from me, energetically whisking the broom around.

I took his response as a yes. "Here," I said, taking the broom from his hand and setting it against the wall, "this'll take just a couple of minutes. You'll thank me for it later, I promise. If you don't like it, you'll never have to do it again."

Dithers got this numb look in his eye, his arm slumped by his side, and he said, "Okay."

I moved in close and put my hand on his hip. I was suddenly conscious that this was the first time we'd touched since I nursed his wound. "Let's try this first," I said. I showed him how to get into position for the Downward Facing Tree pose. "Now envision the roots of your feet slowly growing down into the ground, anchoring you to this spot," I said. I reached down and adjusted the back of his leg, and he laughed. A short, quick "Ha!"

I looked at him like what the hell was that.

"Sorry," he said. "That just felt kind of funny."

We spent the rest of that afternoon going from pose to pose. I showed him how to flow from one to the next. We got all sweaty. There were some obviously embarrassing moments, like when I told him to raise his hands to the sky, but the mood was light, and he forgave my blunders. It was suddenly late. We were having so much fun I decided to skip my Mission for the Good of Mankind that night, and instead we just hung out in between the yoga stuff and rapped about things. Dithers told me that his dad was an albino. And an alcoholic. He said, "It was kind of sad. But I think my dad used to drink to try and forget." Then he told me that when his dad started getting rough with his mother, shoving her around and yelling at her, he'd always step in the way and let his dad beat him instead of his mom. I said that I'd always known he had a good heart, and that story was proof positive. There was a moment of silence.

"I've never told anyone that," said Dithers, looking over at me. I turned and saw the steam coming up off him from all the sweat.

"You're all steamy," I said. I looked over at the chimps in their cages. They were staring back at me, patiently, expectantly.

Dennis cooed, "Hoo-hoo-ha." I realized I hadn't fed them dinner yet.

"Hey, Help People." Dithers slid over a little closer. "I'm sorry, man."

Everything was very quiet. I was getting this weird vibe I couldn't explain.

"For what?"

"For calling you Gay Dad. That G.D. stuff. Back at the base. For giving you such a hard time about all that. That wasn't cool." He said it was probably his insecurity, because of who his own dad was. I tried to envision Dithers as an albino.

Then I told him, don't worry about it, that my dad was a fucking queer, and that I hated his guts for it. "So don't sweat it," I said. "No biggie. Trust me." Then I rolled away from Dithers and grabbed some M.R.E.s and started to feed the chimps their dinner.


## PROPAGANDA LETTER #4

Dear Son,

War sure has changed, and frankly I think whatever dignity used to be in it has been bled out of it by the stupid technology. Last night on *Nightline* they were showing how a little remote-control airplane with a live video feed, an Unmanned Vehicle or something like that, was flying over Saudi Arabia and a bunch of Iraqi soldiers ran up to it waving white flags. The *Nightline* guy kept saying it was a historic moment in warfare, the first time humans surrendered to a machine. And I was thinking, Wow, this is the fourth most powerful army in the world? How do they grade these things, on a bell curve, because I'd sure hate to see the fifth most powerful army in the world. Do you realize that the citizens of Iraq don't even want to be in a war, and that Saddam has forced them into military service, so that when you are killing Iraqi soldiers you are killing innocent people who don't want to be there anyway? I've read in the news that most of the Iraqi soldiers are little boys and old men, what does that tell you? And why is it that our government won't let any journalists in the war theater? Why the censorship? They're denying us the liberty that they claim you're over there defending. Ha!

Rob's been asking me a bunch of questions about my time in Vietnam, and recently I haven't been able to sleep because all these memories keep flooding back. Sometimes I feel like I'm back in the shit all over again, and I can smell the rice paddies and the water buffalo in the bedroom with me. Rob suggested maybe I was being too hard on you. Rob said how do you expect your son to understand where you're coming from when you've never even talked about your own war experiences. When Rob said this, he was holding my Medal of Honor because he'd asked to see it. I know you think I'm a hero, but I want you to know that I'm not. There was nothing heroic about what we did over there. I was a sick young man back then. Sometimes I think Nam is the hangover that Bush is trying to cure by a silly victory over there in Iraq. Because you know in the big picture we got our asses kicked over there, right? Don't let anyone tell you different, the NVA and the Vietcong were the toughest and mightiest warriors that America has ever seen. The government tricked us into fighting that war with all their bullshit about the heroics of WWII. They used words like *evil* and *honor* and dangled our dads in front of us so that we wanted to go over there and be heroes too. We walked into a war that had been going on for twenty years before us and got our asses trounced.

And the things I saw. You'd be out on patrol and come up on a mine site, where some gooks had been blown apart. There'd be pieces of bodies strewn everywhere, arms, legs, half a skull, a torso with the ribs poking out, a kneecap, and the thing is I stopped looking, I didn't even care. What happens to a person when he stops caring? You forgot that the Vietnamese were even people. One time I was crawling through this underground tunnel, because we'd been told there were some NVA officers in there. I heard these voices, all this chattering, and I was thinking, hot damn. So I crawled up the opening where the voices were coming from and chucked a grenade in there and then bam. When I went to inspect the damage, you know what it was, it was a room full of women. They had on some kind of religious costumes. They were all dead. I've got a hundred more stories like that. The things you do in war you have to live with for the rest of your life. How am I supposed to live with something like that? You tell me. How am I.

Dad

## FINALLY THE DAY CAME FOR DITHERS
## TO LEAVE THE BUNKER

Finally the day came for Dithers to leave the bunker. We'd been getting along great for the past couple weeks, and I knew he needed to get his endurance up if he was going to accompany me on my missions. So I suggested we go out and play some catch. To help that arm of his get stronger. We exited the bunker and went about thirty clicks off the highway so that we were out of sight.

"Oh my God," said Dithers when he saw the highway from a distance. Plumes of smoke were trailing up off the smoldering cars.

"See," I said. "Can you smell it?" The barbecue smell was especially strong that day. And then we threw a detonated grenade back and forth. It made me feel like a kid again, and we both laughed, especially because Dithers was having to learn how to throw with his left arm. He looked positively goofy.

"Try to get your hips into it," I shouted at Dithers, after retrieving yet another dud throw from the sand. I looked at Dithers, and he was grinning. The sunlight was catching in his hair. I decided right then and there that we'd make an effort to get out more. I reared back, signaling to Dithers that I was going to really hum this one.

I played all the sports as a kid, but baseball was my favorite. In Little League I played third base for the Fancy Death Life Insurance Bombers. My dad never missed a practice. He'd stand out there in his rope sandals with a couple of the other die-hard parents. And my whole thing was I would pretend I didn't know Dad was there. I'd make a flying leap to stop the ball and whip it to first like a cannon. I'd skin my hip to a pulp sliding into home. Then when I stepped up to the plate I would blow my arms out trying to knock the ball out of the park. I knew a lot of the kids thought I was a jerk. For trying so hard. But I didn't care. This didn't have anything to do with them.

I threw the ball and Dithers dove to catch it, and ended up doing a face plant in the sand. He came up laughing. "Hoo! I don't think I'm going to the big leagues any time soon," he shouted. A breeze picked up and the barbecue smell came up off the highway. I tried not to think about all the rotting corpses out there.

"Here," I said. "Throw me a fly ball. Make me work."

Dithers got to his feet, and then did this little hop-skip, and chucked the grenade way, way up in the air, so that I thought it was going to knock the sun out of the sky.

I remember one game we were getting routed by the fourth inning. Coach moved me from third base to pitcher because he'd used up the other pitchers' eligibility the week before, and because I guess he figured he had nothing to lose. Dad and I always secretly suspected that I'd make a great pitcher; I had a strong arm, and this was my big chance to save the day and show the coach what Dad and I secretly knew: that I should be the starting pitcher. I could almost hear Dad tighten up in the bleachers with excitement as I trotted out to the mound and threw some warm-up pitches. I was really humming them, and I could feel the world smiling at me, claiming me for one of its marvelous creatures. I touched the bill of my cap. I wet the tip of my fingers with my tongue. I blazed a couple more fastballs across the plate for good measure. Then the umpire shouted, "Play ball." And for the rest of that inning, until we had to forfeit, I've never felt more shame in my life. I threw wild ball after wild ball. I walked six batters straight. And when I wasn't throwing wild, the other team was connecting with everything I threw. Even their benchwarmers were getting a piece of me.

I sprinted after Dithers's fly ball and leapt and stretched out, my body soaring parallel to the ground, and there was the smack of the grenade as it landed in my palm. I crashed into the sand, victorious.

"Damn," shouted Dithers. "Awesome."

I stood up and waved the grenade like a trophy. I took a bow.

"I'd give you a standing ovation but," and he nodded at his shoulder, "you know the whole sound-of-one-hand-clapping thing."

My face was flushed, and I felt the thrill of the catch rush through my body. I felt like running into the highway and picking up a tank and throwing it.

"Hey," said Dithers, trotting up to me. "That was really fucking amazing. Did you used to play ball or what?"

All the blood rushed out of my face. I felt the crushing reality of our situation set back in. I wanted to puke because of that smoky smell. All those dead people. If I ran out into the highway, I'd probably just get run over. Suddenly Rob's mustached face was hovering there in front of me. *Which one is it? Are you going to kick my ass? Or are you going to stick my head up my ass? Because I don't know how my head would fit up my ass if you are busy kicking it.* Then I heard my faggot dad's laugh.

"Naw," I said to Dithers, turning to head back to the bunker. "I never did get to play. I always wanted to though."

After my humiliating pitching experience, I couldn't stop crying on the drive home. There was a purple can of grape pop in my lap that I hadn't even bothered to open. I was crying because I was so embarrassed that I was crying. Dad had this tight look on his face and he didn't say a word the whole time. I could tell he wasn't upset; he just felt my pain and knew there was nothing he could say to make it better. When we pulled into the driveway and the car came to a stop, he squeezed me on the shoulder and said, "We don't have to try and explain this to your mom. You go in and get washed up. But I don't care what happened out there. I'm proud of you. Do you hear me? You are my son. Don't ever forget that."


## THE DAYS BEGAN TO BLUR

The days began to blur, and it got so I couldn't remember life any other way. There were more and more Iraqis on the highway at night, trying to make it back to Baghdad. Some nights I'd tend to as many as three people. My only concern was the M.R.E.s. We still had plenty, but between me and Dithers, and the chimpanzees, we'd already run through half the box. Dithers and I fell into a routine of doing yoga together in the evening, right before I'd head out for the night. Dithers was a natural. Sometimes I'd inadvertently come out of the void because I lost my concentration, and I'd look over and Dithers would be crouched down, holding the Half Moon pose, with this very serene look on his face. I have to admit I was a little jealous.

But one time I opened my eyes, and Dithers was standing right in front of me with a grin on his face. I tried to hide my surprise.

"Dithers," I said. I didn't know what else to say. "Hi."

"Hey," he said. "I want you to show me that one pose you do."

I said I didn't know what he was talking about. He was right up in my face, all smiles.

"You know the one. Where you lay down like this." He got down on the ground facefirst. He looked idiotic.

"You mean the Half Locust?" I lay down in the Half Locust.

"Yeah," he said, grinning even wider. So I showed him. I put my arms around him, guiding his limbs into the correct posture. I knelt beside him as he lay there.

"But what about this part here?" he said. "This doesn't feel right," pointing to his hip.

"Looks right to me," I said. I reached down under him and before I knew what was happening, Dithers had adjusted himself so that my hand was cupping his groin area. I got a very strange feeling in my stomach. An odd sensation. His hand came up around my neck and pulled me to him, very hard. It felt aggressive. "Help me, Help People," he murmured, but there was some menace in his voice and my hand was pinned between his groin and the ground. I felt things spinning out of control, and that weird feeling had bloomed so that it was running through my entire body.

"Help me, Help People," only this time louder, meaner. Like a growl.

I swung my elbow around and clipped his jaw and then leapt to my feet.

"What the fuck," I shouted. The chimps joined in, baring their teeth and hooting.

Dithers looked genuinely surprised to see me on my feet. He was rolling his jaw around. I noticed he had an ammo can in his hand, which he tossed away.

"I'm sorry," he said, getting to his feet. "I don't know what that was. I think it's the stress. Maybe being cooped up down here is starting to get to me. My bad. Okay. I'm sorry. No problem, right?"

I was confused. I didn't want to know what any of this meant. I couldn't quite get my mind around what had just happened, and the confusion turned to anger. I looked at the chimps and wanted to chop their heads off. They started hooting and screeching, as if they could read my thoughts.

I threw the broom at Dithers and said, "Here. This place is a fucking mess."

## A QUICK CLARIFICATION,
## BEFORE WE GO ANY FURTHER

No matter what I may be accused of, I'm definitely not gay. I want to put that right out there. The closest I've ever come to being gay was in the fourth grade. And that was a long time ago. I mean, to be perfectly honest with you, my fourth-grade year was probably the gayest year of my life. That was the year that I spent each recess out on the corner of the playground playing Truth or Dare. And on the fateful day in late spring, Freddie Slacknit produced a carrot he'd smuggled from the cafeteria, and double-dog dared me to stick it up his "pooper." At first I didn't know what to do. The other kids looked at me expectantly, and Freddie already had his pants down around his ankles. I almost walked away. But in the end Freddie had to go to the school nurse to get the carrot out, and by the next day word of what had happened spread through the Parent Majority Coalition and somehow I was being pegged as "the ringleader." The kids at school started calling me Rabbit Butt. They'd spank themselves and start howling when I walked by. Secret PMC meetings were held. Teenagers from the high school drove by and hummed carrots and lettuce heads at our house. Four months later it was so bad we had to move to a house on the other side of Raleigh, and I transferred schools. That was a long time ago. So obviously I didn't feel compelled to mention any of this to my recruiter when he asked me if I was gay.

## PROPAGANDA LETTER #5

Dear Son,

This is going to be hard for me to talk about, but I am doing it for you, so that you recognize how empty the pursuit of killing other human beings is. I hope that by the time you're done reading this you will realize what a hollow word *bravery* is in the context of war. I wore the craziness of the war like a cheap suit and sealed the lock from the inside so I couldn't get out even when I wanted to. One day we were on patrol, near the town Dak Tho in the province of Quang Mgai. We'd gotten word there might be some NVA in the area, and so we were roving through the banyan trees and bamboo thickets. Suddenly Charlie caught us in an ambush. My buddy Kitrick fell into a tiger pit. He yelled, "Fuck," and then the light went out of his eyes. We're suddenly taking a lot of fire, and I'm scared and confused. We scrambled for cover, and Gordon got his leg shot to shit. I bent over to check the wound, and Gordon moved and something blew up in my face and I was blind. I heard screams and I knew the VC were moving in on us. I wiped my eyes and there was blood on my hands but I could see, and then I ran out into this little clearing and started blasting with my pistol. There were five dinks total, and there was a split second where we all looked at one another and the colors were ultra-vivid and it was as if we were onstage and this was the scene we'd all been waiting for and then the pistol was guiding my hand, jerking it around dropping them out. When I was done I started calling out for our guys to come up, but it was quiet. The wind was coming through the banyan trees and it was almost pretty. Everyone dead except for me.

That's how I got my Medal of Honor. Two more tours and my mind just shut off and I didn't even think about the killing and I wondered about that later. My mind was a blank slate. When I rotated back to the world, I had to pick up a piece of chalk and start writing my new life story with it. I'm sorry to be having to tell you this and for you to know it about me.

I'm not the same person I was back then, son. Read Chomsky.

As ever,<br>Dad

## HOW OUR COVER WAS ALMOST BLOWN

A couple days after that strange yoga incident, I was returning to the bunker when I spotted a lone figure in the distance. A human dot on the landscape. There'd been a lot of Republican Guards in the area recently, making my night missions more difficult. The sun was just starting to dawn, a bloodred symphony of light, playing its chorus of hope over the horizon. I was worried this figure was some Iraqi soldier snooping around the hatch to my bunker. Maybe he'd sat on the boulder and saw the shine of the metal underneath. I didn't know what I'd do if that were the case. Should I sneak up behind the Iraqi and club him with a rock? What would I do with him then, drag him down into the bunker for questioning? But I wouldn't be able to question him because I don't speak Arabic, so then what? Just keep him in the extra cage? What would Dithers think? Plus surely he'd be missed. How long would I keep him in the cage, because it's not as if we had all the food in the world? We were already starting to run out of M.R.E.s. And it didn't seem right for me to hurt someone who was sneaking around. But then again, it didn't seem right for me to be discovered and captured. Because who would care for the wounded pilgrims then? So I got down in the sand and speed-crawled up very quietly on the Iraqi in a roundabout fashion, until he was about thirty yards away.

I raised my binoculars to my eyes and I was relieved to see that it was only Dithers. In the binoculars he was suddenly close, and I could see a drop of sweat dangling from the tip of his nose. By now he was walking very fast alongside the highway and kept checking over his shoulder. He was headed north. I wondered if maybe one of the chimps had escaped and he was trying to catch it. I knew Dennis had been acting funny recently. But how could Dennis get out? I realized that Dithers was not in the underground bunker, which is where he said he would stay, and I realized that if Dithers were in the underground bunker, there was no way Dennis could get out.

I stood up. "Dithers," I called. "What are you doing?"

I guess he couldn't hear me because he didn't turn around. So I called out again.

"Dithers!"

He turned and saw me.

I waved.

Now this is the part that left me stunned and heartbroken. When Dithers saw me he started running in the opposite direction from where I was. I realized right then and there that if Dithers made it back he'd rat me out. All of his previous questions suddenly came flooding back into my mind. *What exactly are our coordinates? Is there a landmark you use to know where the underground bunker is? Do you ever get lost?* And there was no way I was going to the brig. My only crime was my compassion. It was easy to catch him. Even with my limp. I tackled him.

## PROPAGANDA LETTER #6

Dear Son,

    I have a confession to make. I didn't want to tell you this, but Rob encouraged me to come completely clean with you. He said if I was being all high and mighty with you, then I had to lead by example, so I am going to come clean. I want you to know the truth about your mom. Now I know you were never close to your mom, because of the language thing, and because she tragically passed away when you were eight, and it's true I often expressed my disappointment in her to you. I shouldn't have done that. And sometimes you may wonder why I stayed with her all that time. Especially if I was so unhappy. The answer is because of the guilt I felt. When I met your mom she was a green-eyed ten-dollar whore in China Beach. My team was on a twenty-four-hour R&R. We didn't have any language to share, your mom and I, so we communicated through clumsy, passionate hand signals, under the sheets. And when the weekend was over, your mom stood at the edge of town in a red, white, and blue straw shawl and waved good-bye to me as our jeep pulled out, her head full of my empty promises that I passed on to her through a translator. That I would return soon in a giant yacht named *O Powerful One* to marry her and bring her back with me to America, where we would live in a gold mansion. But as you well know, I did come back for her. And though her life was sad and strange, I am always grateful to her for having given me you. I didn't mean what I said earlier, about you being the worst mistake I ever made. Sometimes I get angry and lose my cool.

    As you can probably tell, Rob's a pretty good influence on me and keeps me walking a straight line, and what once started as an ironic gesture, with this protest, which I still stand by, has become very serious. I think I am in love. Did I mention that

Rob isn't circumcised? I'll admit that freaked me out at first. It looked so silly to me, but now I've grown used to it and sometimes when I look down at my own unit I wish it wasn't circumcised, because Rob says he gets more pleasure that way, and based on the noises he makes I believe him. But all that aside, I'm ashamed of the way you acted when you came over here and started yelling right before you shipped out. Now I realize this can't be easy for you, but you're going to have to trust me on this one. Homophobia is one of the ugliest things on earth, and it stems from ignorance and fear. All I am trying to say is I hope you will give Rob another chance. He's a really good man. And he's got an interesting past, can you believe he grew up in London? And he said he has forgiven you for your rudeness and looks forward to really getting to know you.
I know if you would just give him a chance the two of you could maybe become friends. I hope you will consider this while you are over there, and realize that I am finally happy after all these years and that should stand for something. Happiness is not easily come by in this world.

Love,
Dad

## DITHERS WAS BACK IN THE CAGE
## FULL-TIME NOW

Dithers was back in the cage full-time now. And I began to see him for what he truly was, a liar, a conniver, a coward. He started having these mood swings and shouting a lot. "Let me out of here, I won't tell anyone you're here. I promise. I just have to get back to the guys. My mom will be worried about me. Can't you understand what that's like? Please." Then he'd start crying. Other times he'd turn angry and violent. "Help People, I'm going to kill you. Your days are numbered, Help People. See this bare hand?" And here he held up his one arm. "I'm going to kill you with my bare hand."

## WRESTLING AS A FORM OF CONNECTION, AND AS A PREVENTIVE MEASURE AGAINST POSSIBLE FUTURE ATTACKS

The only time I let the chimps out of their cages is when we wrestle. This was my idea too. Not Dithers's. I thought it was good for the chimps to have physical contact. Dithers didn't seem to care for the chimps one way or another. He wouldn't even acknowledge they were there. Like he was better than them or something. Lots of times I'd see that they were lonely and go over and talk to the chimps and make funny faces. But not Dithers. And beating a chimpanzee in a wrestling match gave me confidence, and I knew if I could take a chimpanzee then Dithers wouldn't have a chance against me if he ever did try anything. Dithers's one arm was a trunk, and I'd seen him doing all those push-ups. But you go five rounds with Dennis and a little guy like Dithers becomes a joke. Even with the trunk. That's why I always wrestled the chimps right in front of Dithers's cage, where he couldn't miss any of the action. Every fight is 80 percent intimidation. So I made it my business to psych Dithers out before he made his move.

A couple days ago, while wrestling with Ronald, I got myself in a pinch. I was crouched down low, circling around with my arms spread kung-fu style, when suddenly I slipped on an ammo can and fell over backward. The bunker has gotten real messy with Dithers in the cage all the time. Ronald leapt on me and started punching me everywhere at once. I was surprised. There'd always been a playful undertone about the wrestling matches, but Ronald wasn't holding back. He knocked the wind out of me. He stomped on my bad knee, and I saw a hairy fist in front of my face. Blood came spurting out of my nose. I heard, as if from very far away, the chimpanzees start screeching. Then there was the unmistakable sound of Dithers's cackling. My vision went foggy under Ronald's little concrete fists. Boom boom boom boom boom. I decided I needed to do something because this situation was about to turn very bad for me, and then I blacked out.

When I came to I saw Ronald poised with an empty ammo can raised over my head. I quickly slid out from under him and flipped Ronald over on his back and then pinned his shoulders to the ground with my knees. I punched Ronald hard in the face and he went limp. Then I looked up at Dithers and shouted, "You want some of this? You want some of this? Come on then! Come and get some, Dithers, motherfucker!" But as soon as I said it I knew I'd crossed a line and I felt pretty bad about the whole thing, and I tried to apologize to him later.

Beverly's the best wrestler. She's got a headlock that could crush a shark. Chimpanzees are five times stronger than human beings. So when I beat one of the chimpanzees like that, I have to wonder if I'm something better than a human being. Some sort of superhuman being.

## THE DEBILITATING CONUNDRUM OF FOOD AS AN ENERGY SOURCE

Despite my impressive defeat over Ronald, this situation with Dithers only got worse over the next couple days. It was highly unpleasant. And it worried me too. Because when I left the underground bunker at night I wondered if Dithers would be able to get out. I always checked the lock on his cage before I left, but you never knew. I wasn't free to be my new self anymore. My identity as Help People was being compromised by

Dithers. I didn't understand how he could do this to me considering how I'd saved his life and helped him rehabilitate his arm. And how could I devote myself to giving medical attention to the innocent victims of war when I was worried that this maniac Dithers was going to be there waiting to crush my skull when I came back to the bunker in the morning?

And to make matters worse, it was about this time that our food rations started to run out. Even though I'd carefully rationed out our M.R.E.s they were dwindling fast, and then one day they were gone. There was no more. I felt bad about this, because I knew how hungry the chimpanzees and Dithers were getting. And that didn't seem fair. But I have always been resourceful, and soon after that I started catching lizards for food. There are these little pink lizards that skate around on the concrete walls of the bunker and disappear in the cracks. The lizards are translucent, and you can see their tiny skeletons under their skin. Their eyes are almost half as big as their bodies and look like Tic-Tacs. About the only thing you can't see is their thoughts.

## MY EFFORT TO ELIMINATE ANYTHING THAT POSED A THREAT TO MY NEWFOUND MISSION

Catching enough lizards to feed two men and five chimpanzees takes a lot of time, and I found that I was sleeping less and less. I tried to catch catnaps here and there. But I was starting to see lizards in my dreams. Then I started to dream that I was a lizard. I would scurry around on all four legs and people would laugh at me because they could see my insides. Until finally I just quit sleeping altogether. I found that I didn't need to sleep. Now I haven't slept in weeks, and it seems strange to me that this was something that I ever did.

## INCARCERATION AS A FORM OF REHABILITATION, BECAUSE I REMAINED HOPEFUL AND OPTIMISTIC

And I still didn't know what to do about Dithers, but I hadn't given up hope on him yet. I was confused but optimistic. Sometimes it's hard to make someone see the light. I was crushed because I felt like all my hard work was down the tubes. I tried my best to come up with ways for him to like our new life here. I told him to look inside his heart. I told him I wanted him to be able to come out with me at night on the missions. I was getting tired of witnessing all the atrocities of war alone. I begged and pleaded with him to consider my position in all this. He'd yell at me. I clapped my hands over my ears. But still I didn't give up. I even offered to let him do some yoga with me. I told him I'd let him out of the cage if he wanted to do some yoga. He kept yelling. I told him how he was just becoming like his alcoholic dad. I told him, don't be that way.

"You're not an albino. You're not an albino," I said.

And then Dithers began to show the true darkness in his heart. He was talking all the time. Nonstop. Every time I tried to do some yoga. Shouting at me. Yoga was out of the question, and I started to lose my internal balance. It was a racket. I couldn't think straight. The void was slipping further and further away. It was like garbage can lids banging in my head. Taunting me. Heckling me. Calling me Gay Dad. Gay Dad. I'd come back to the bunker and lie down with my hands over my ears. Gay Dad. Gay Dad. Gay Dad. Gay Dad.

## WHAT HAPPENED WHEN THE LIZARDS RAN OUT, AND THE PURSUIT OF ALTERNATIVE ENERGY SOURCES

The lizards ran out. At some point I realized there weren't any lizards left. Dithers saw me scrabbling around for lizards and realized what had happened and started laughing. "Great, what are you going to do now, Gay Dad? I'm hungry!" he shouted. But then Dithers said a curious thing.

He whispered ever so softly, "Eat me."

I turned on him. "What did you just say?"

"Eat me. I'm delicious. I taste good."

That time I knew exactly what I'd heard. I said, "Why did you just tell me to eat you, Dithers?"

He got this funny look on his face.

"Shut the hell up. I didn't say anything. I haven't said a word since you got back. I'm being good for once. What the hell are you talking about?"

But then he followed that up with his whisper again: "Eat me. Eat me. Eat me. I'm yummy. Look at this arm of mine. This arm looks delicious."

I turned and looked at his arm.

"What the hell are you looking at," he said.

"Don't worry yourself about it. No need to play games. I heard you the first time, Dithers."

I went back to scrounging around in my rucksack, but then in an instant I knew exactly what I was going to do. I went to the back of the bunker. The chimps were hissing and shouting. Dithers was screaming. Then I picked up an empty ammo can and started for Dithers's cage.

## MY DAD'S FINAL PROPAGANDA LETTER, WHICH I RECEIVED THE DAY BEFORE I SCOOPED UP DITHERS AND QUIT THE WAR

Dear Son,

The idea that I have fathered a son who wants to kill other human beings in the name of his country breaks my heart. I am begging you please don't do the things I did, you will regret them for the rest of your life, I promise you. Man is not made to relish pain in others and it is the sickness of war that propagates this belief, and we have to hold on to what makes us human, and not revert back to the life of animals. I butchered human beings and killing became a pleasure. I do not want for you to suffer the black scars on your soul that I have on mine because of Vietnam please listen to me I am not joking anymore this is the most serious thing I have ever said to you, you are my son and don't ever forget that.

Dad

## THE INEVITABLE LIBERATION OF DITHERS

I flung open Dithers's cage and swung the ammo can at his head and missed. The chimps were banging on the slats of their cages and screeching, and in the chaos I closed my eyes and focused and swung again, this time it was different though, this time I swung with the confidence and ease of a man who knows it's going to be a home run. I opened my eyes. Dithers's cage was empty. In that split second I was shoved from behind and heard the ominous click of the lock as the cage door slammed shut. I whirled and crashed into the slats and fell over. Dithers was beaming. For the next half hour as I calmly stared out through the slats while seething with outrage, Dithers went around the bunker packing my ruck with stuff for his journey, informing me as to how he was going to grab Marty and the guys and that they'd be back to beat the living shit out of me and then flexcuff me and ship my ass to the brig. "The game's up, Mr. Fucking Asshole Freak. I sure hope you like those bars, cuz you're gonna be seeing a lot more of them from here on out," said Dithers, and then he breezed out of sight, and I heard the hatch swing open and then slam to. A half hour later I finally jimmied open the lock with a paper clip from my pocket, and sprinted out of the bunker and out into the night, scanning the horizon desperately for Dithers. I searched all up and down the highway for the next several hours until the sun came up, ignoring the wounded Iraqi boy who called out to me as I raced past. But Dithers was gone.

And then today I came back and paced around the bunker, consumed with bitterness and rage and a deep sense of betrayal, but I finally caught my snap and moved past that, realizing that these emotions were of no use to me. I realized that Dithers did what he did not because he's a hateful person, but because he's simply misguided. And, most important, I found confirmation that I was a good person. And then tonight, exhausted but with a renewed sense of resolve, I started to go out on my mission for the Good of Mankind, with hardly any of my stuff because Dithers had stolen it all, and I reached for the handle on the hatch but it was stuck. I shook it harder, but it wouldn't budge. Then I heard Marty's snickering voice call out, "Hey, what's going on down there, *Help People.*" A chorus of laughter erupted, and I could tell there was a bunch of them up there. I heard Dithers's distinctive cackle. "Hoo! What's amatter, can't get outta there! Hey, whadya know, there's a boulder up here! Ha-ha!" Then Diaz called out in a low voice that rose as he went on, "Hey, help help. Help me, Help People! Help help!," and then they all chimed in and were roaring it together, over and over, "Hey, help help. Help me, Help People! Help! Help!"

And it hurts, because they don't know this but I really would, I'd rescue each and every one of them if they needed it. There's no ocean or stretch of land I wouldn't cross to save their lives, and here they are, just fifteen feet away, doing everything they can to keep me from it.

## ACKNOWLEDGMENTS

Much gratitude to the following people: Chris Rhodes, Jenny Minton, Ira Silverberg, Deborah Treisman, Dave Eggers, Bill Buford, Paul Maliszewski, Robert Coover, Ben Marcus, Lynne Tillman, Elena Wealty, Megan Hustad, Jesse Dorris, Jorge Hernandez, Hank Denault, Lola Denault, Peter Semere, Virginia Ewing Hudson, my younger brother Kendall, and most of all to Sarah Raymont, for the storm.

PREVIOUS PUBLICATIONS

The following stories first appeared in other publications:

"The American Green Machine" appeared in *Conjunctions Web*.

"Dear Mr. President" appeared in slightly different form in *The New Yorker*.

"Cross-Dresser" and "General Schwarzkopf Looks Back at His Humble Beginning" (in slightly different form) appeared in *McSweeney's*.

"Those Were Your Words Not Mine" appeared in *Columbia: A Journal of Literature and Art*.

A NOTE ABOUT THE AUTHOR

Gabe Hudson was a rifleman in the Marine Reserves. He received an MFA from Brown University, where he won the 1999 John Hawkes Prize in Fiction. His stories have been published in *The New Yorker* and *McSweeney's*. He lives in New York City.

A NOTE ON THE TYPE

This book was set in Caledonia, a Linotype face designed by W. A. Dwiggins (1880–1956). It belongs to the family of printing types called "modern face" by printers—a term used to mark the change in style of the type letters that occurred around 1800. Caledonia borders on the general design of Scotch Roman but it is more freely drawn than that letter.

Composed by Creative Graphics,
Allentown, Pennsylvania
Printed and bound by R. R. Donnelly & Sons,
Harrisonburg, Virginia
Designed by Virginia Tan